"You really have a gorgeous body, Chip,"
Jill murmured shyly.

"Lord," he said, wiping a line of perspiration off his brow with his thumb. "You shouldn't say things like that."

"Why not? It's true."

"But it shakes up my libido."

"Really?" Jill smiled. "Sorry about that." But her eyes held no regret.

"Jill, I'd better go now, while I still can. I want to kiss you good-bye." He leaned forward without waiting for her response and brushed his lips across Jill's in a fleeting motion. In the next instant he gathered her to his chest as she wrapped her arms around his neck, inching her fingertips into his thick hair.

Desire started to glow deep within her, bringing a soft moan from her throat. New sensations swirled unchecked from the tips of her toes to the flush on her cheeks as she returned Chip's kiss in total abandonment. Acutely aware of her femininity, Jill rejoiced in the knowledge for the first time. . . .

WHAT ARE *LOVESWEPT* ROMANCES?

They are stories of true romance and touching emotion. We believe those two very important ingredients are constants in our highly sensual and very believable stories in the *LOVESWEPT* line. Our goal is to give you, the reader, stories of consistently high quality that may sometimes make you laugh, sometimes make you cry, but are always fresh and creative and contain many delightful surprises within their pages.

Most romance fans read an enormous number of books. Those they truly love, they keep. Others may be traded with friends and soon forgotten. We hope that each *LOVESWEPT* romance will be a treasure—a "keeper." We will always try to publish

LOVE STORIES YOU'LL NEVER FORGET
BY AUTHORS YOU'LL ALWAYS REMEMBER

The Editors

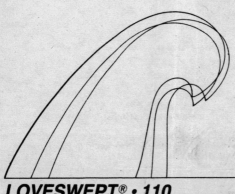

LOVESWEPT® • 110
Joan Elliott Pickart
Sunlight's Promise

 BANTAM BOOKS
TORONTO · NEW YORK · LONDON · SYDNEY · AUCKLAND

SUNLIGHT'S PROMISE

A Bantam Book / September 1985

LOVESWEPT® and the wave device are registered trademarks of Bantam Books, Inc. Registered in U.S. Patent and Trademark Office and elsewhere.

ISBN 0-553-21719-4

Published simultaneously in the United States and Canada

PRINTED IN THE UNITED STATES OF AMERICA

O   0 9 8 7 6 5 4 3 2 1

For Ricky

One

William Robert Chandler, Jr., known to his friends and family as Chip, stepped into the lobby of the building and welcomed the warmth that greeted him. A chill wind was blowing off the Detroit River, making the morning air even more damp and cold.

"Morning, Mr. Chandler," the security guard on duty said. "Bit nasty outside."

"Typical February, Joe," Chip said, unbuttoning his sheepskin jacket. "Mr. Jenkins come in yet?"

" 'Bout half hour ago. Don't see why you two young fellas have to work on a Saturday."

"It's the only way we can keep up. Vestco is growing and, believe me, we're not complaining."

"Yeah, well, in my day, Saturdays were for courtin' the ladies."

Chip laughed. "There's always tonight. See you later."

Walking to the bank of elevators, he punched the button and shoved his hands into the pockets of his jacket. A frown crossed his face, pulling his dark eyebrows together. The black-tie affair he was going to attend that evening held no appeal, nor did the woman he was attending it with. Brenda would be her usual beautiful self, but would chatter constantly about nothing of interest. Chip would plaster on a plastic smile and try to ignore the fact that Brenda was grating on his nerves.

His reverie was cut short by the elevator doors swishing open, and he stepped in, automatically pressing the button for the seventh floor. Only then did he notice that the enclosure was completely dark.

Wonderful, he thought as the elevator started slowly upward. The light must be burned out. Security guard or not, downtown Detroit was not the place to be riding in a dark elevator. He'd call Joe from the office and tell him that the—

"Excuse me," a quiet voice said.

"Huh?" Chip said, spinning around.

"I—I think I'm going to faint and I thought I'd warn you so you wouldn't have a heart attack or anything. I'm—Oh!"

Instinctively Chip reached out, and a small bundle in a wool jacket tumbled into his arms. He swung his unexpected cargo up against his chest, one arm about her shoulders, the other under her legs. As the doors to the elevator swished open, he stepped out into the brightly lit corridor and stared down at the limp figure he held.

"A girl!" he said. "Oh, man, now what do I do?"

He strode quickly down the hallway to a door that boasted the name "Vestco." Bending slightly he turned the knob and entered the thickly carpeted reception area, kicking the door shut with his foot.

"R.J.!" he hollered.

"What?" a voice called.

"Come in my office. Quick!"

Chip walked into a large room and gently laid the

unmoving girl on a leather sofa, tucking a throw pillow under her head.

"R.J.!"

"I'm here. What's all the commotion about? Half the city can hear you and—What have you done? You brought a dead body in here?"

"No, she fainted on me in the elevator," Chip said, shrugging out of his jacket.

"Cataledge," the girl mumbled.

"Cataledge?" R.J. said. "Never heard of him. You suppose that's who she was on her way to see?"

"Check the building directory," Chip said. "See if there's anyone named Cataledge listed."

"She sure is pretty, Chip. How old do you think she is?"

"How should I know?" he said, sitting down on the sofa next to the girl. "Just look up Cataledge, will you?"

"Yeah, okay," R.J. said, moving behind Chip's desk.

"Hello? Hello?" Chip said, patting the girl's hand.

"Cataledge," she mumbled again, but did not open her eyes.

"We're getting him, honey," Chip said. "Try to wake up." What a lovely face, he thought. Like a pixie. Her hair was so dark and shiny, two thick braids hanging over the front of her coat. Long eyelashes fluttered, then slowly lifted to reveal large green eyes. "Hi," Chip said. "Feeling better?"

"I . . . Who . . . What . . . Oh!" the girl said, attempting to sit up.

"Hey, take it easy," Chip said, pushing her gently back by the shoulders. "What's your name?"

"Jill."

"Jill?"

"Tinsley. Jill Tinsley. I'm awfully warm."

"Oh, sure. Here, let's get that jacket off," Chip said, reaching for the buttons.

"I'll manage," Jill said, sitting up and removing her pea jacket.

Not a kid, he thought, his eyes flickering over the full breasts pushing against the faded rose-colored sweater. Most definitely not a kid. That was a mature woman staring at him with those gorgeous green eyes.

"I'm sorry for the fuss," Jill said, sinking back onto the pillow. Good grief, she thought, what a beautiful man! Thick dark hair, yummy velvet brown eyes, handsome features, and those shoulders! Just absolutely beautiful. He must have carried her when she'd fainted. Darn, she'd missed being held in those strong arms.

"No one named Cataledge," R.J. said, coming back over to the sofa. "Hello, Sleeping Beauty. I'm glad you could join the party. I heard you say your name is Jill Tinsley. I'm Roger Jenkins, but call me R.J."

"Hello," Jill said, smiling. The expression seemed to light up her entire face.

"I'm Chip Chandler," Chip said quickly. "We can't seem to locate your Mr. Cataledge."

Jill looked puzzled. "Who?"

"You said his name," Chip said. "We thought maybe you were in the building to see him, but R.J. couldn't find him in the directory."

"Cataledge?" Jill said. "Oh, I understand. No, you see, I meant 'cat on the ledge.' There's a cat on the ledge outside a window on this floor and it looks so frightened. I was hoping to be able to rescue it."

"Oh, man," R.J. said, bursting into laughter.

"How did you get past the security guard?" Chip asked. "No one is allowed upstairs in this building on weekends without clearance."

"I told him I was pregnant and was having morning sickness and just had to use the restroom. Then I circled around and went to the elevator. It was going down instead of up, though, and you got on when it stopped at the first floor again."

"Are you? I mean, is that why you fainted?" Chip asked. Hell, it was none of his business, he thought, but still . . .

"That's none of your business," R.J. said.

"Oh, I'm not pregnant." She laughed and the sound seemed to dance across Chip's spine.

"That's nice," he said, smiling at Jill as R.J. looked at him curiously.

"It's about the cat," Jill said.

"Right," Chip said, pushing himself to his feet. "You stay put. R.J. and I will have a look out the window."

"We will?" R.J. said. "Hey, I'm not crawling out on any ledge after some—"

"Can't hurt to look," Chip said, walking across the room. "Come on."

Jill turned to watch as the two men opened the window. They were almost the same height, about six feet tall, and had the nicely muscled physiques of athletes, with wide shoulders and narrow hips. R. J. was as fair as Chip was dark, and both had healthy tans.

A dynamic duo, Jill thought. But as good-looking as R. J. was, there was something about Chip Chandler that intrigued her. He was so big and strong, but there had been tenderness, concern, and warmth in the depth of his brown eyes. He might be thirty years old, but when he had smiled his face had taken on a boyish quality, a beguiling charm. And, brother, did he know how to fill out a pair of faded jeans.

"There it is," Chip said over his shoulder as he leaned out the window. "Here, kitty, kitty. Damn, it's just sitting there shaking all over."

"Let me try," R.J. said. "Hey, Cataledge! Get your tush in here! Nope. He won't budge."

"Excuse me," Jill said, easing between the two men.

"Jill, you shouldn't be up," Chip said. "You might get dizzy again."

"I'm fine. Oh, look at that poor baby," she said, poking her head out the window.

"Jill, it's cold out there. Put your coat on," Chip said.

"Who are you? Her father?" R.J. asked, and was rewarded with a stormy glare from Chip.

"Come on, sweetheart," Jill crooned. "You don't want to be out there all alone in the cold. How did you get up here in the first place, Cataledge? Do you like that name? I think it suits you. That's it, just a little farther. Easy now. There! Ta-*da*," she said, emerging from the window with a cat that was various shades of gray and black and had a white stripe down its nose. "Gentlemen, meet Cataledge."

"Sick-looking cat," R.J. muttered.

"She's cute," Jill said, nuzzling her nose in the animal's fur. "Uh-oh."

"What's wrong?" Chip yelled. "Are you dizzy? R.J., close the window."

"Cripes," R.J. said, slamming it back into place. "Anything else, doctor?"

"Stow it. Jill?"

"It's Cataledge. Look at her tummy. She's pregnant."

"That's it. I'm gone," R.J. said. "Chip, I finished the figures on the Hunt account and I'm off to lunch with an extremely lovely acquaintance of mine. Hope you're feeling better, Jill. Drop by again sometime. See ya, Cataledge, you naughty girl you."

"Good-bye, R.J.," Jill said. "Thank you."

"See ya," Chip said absently as R.J. left the room.

"I'd better be going too," Jill said. "I really do appreciate everything you—"

"No! I mean, you should rest some more. People don't faint for no reason."

"I know why I conked out," Jill said, reaching for

her coat. "I just need a little food in my stomach. Well, thanks again and—"

"When did you eat last?"

"Yesterday."

"When yesterday?"

"Early. Good-bye, Chip."

"Jill, wait. Why don't we go out and get some lunch or breakfast?"

"No, I don't think so."

"Why not?"

"Because . . . I really don't know you."

"Sure you do," he said, smiling at her. "I'm the guy whose arms you fainted into, remember? We're way past being strangers. I've only had a couple cups of coffee this morning and I'm ready for a meal. Okay?" Dammit, he thought, why was he pushing it? If she didn't want to go, forget it. But why hadn't she eaten? Was she a bubblehead who lost track of time or was she broke? Never in his life had he seen such incredible green eyes on a woman. She had a way of looking at a person that was damn unsettling, as if she'd know in an instant if she were being conned. And that face. Lovely. Absolutely lovely.

"Well . . ." Jill said. "What about Cataledge?"

"We'll leave her in the car and bring her a doggie bag or cat bag or whatever. What do you say?"

Yes? No? Jill wondered. She *was* very hungry. And another hour in Chip Chandler's company? How nice. He was, without a doubt, the most masculine man she had ever encountered. He emanated sexuality just walking across the room. And yet he was so kind. "All right," she said.

"Great. Let's go."

He assisted her with her jacket while she shifted a now purring Cataledge from arm to arm. The cat was dozing by the time Jill and Chip emerged from the elevator in the lobby.

"There you are, little lady," Joe said. "You must

have been feeling mighty poorly. You sure was gone a long time."

"I'm fine now, thank you," Jill said.

"You know this little girl, Mr. Chandler?"

"We're old friends," Chip said. "Bye, Joe. Oh, the light is out in the elevator. Better have it fixed. Never know what might pop out at a person."

"Oh, thanks," Jill said.

"I'll take care of it," Joe said.

"And," Jill said, when she and Chip were out on the sidewalk, "I am not a 'little girl.' "

"Maybe," Chip said, tugging on one of her braids, "Joe was only referring to your lack of height, because, Miss Tinsley, you are definitely a woman."

"Well, thank you, sir. I suppose the pigtails don't help my cause, but I was in a hurry. Besides, at five foot two I'm not that short. Men like you just happen to be very tall."

"Of course." He nodded solemnly. "My car is right down the block. Let's hurry and get inside before we freeze to death."

Chip's car was a bronze-colored late-model sedan and Jill ran her hand over the soft material of the seat while Chip slid behind the wheel.

"This is a lovely car," she said as he pulled away from the curb.

"I had a little sports number, but I decided it was time to get a larger, roomier car. How's Cataledge doing?"

"She's sound asleep. I still can't figure out how she got out on that window ledge."

"I'm glad she managed it," he said quietly. "Otherwise we never would have met."

Jill glanced up quickly to look at Chip, but he was concentrating on his driving. She studied his profile, the firm line of his jaw, the straight nose, the thick dark hair combed over his ears and falling to the collar of his jacket. His hands were large with long fingers, and she could see how his thigh muscles moved beneath the soft denim as his foot shifted from the accelerator to the brake. He was, Jill decided again, absolutely beautiful. As her heart began to dance a strange little beat, she tore her gaze from Chip Chandler's massive frame and stared down at Cataledge.

"How can you have a tan in the dead of winter?" she asked, hoping her voice sounded steady.

"R.J. and I went skiing. There's a restaurant up ahead that's nothing fancy but the food is excellent. They have homemade biscuits that are out of this world."

"Sounds great."

"I'm going to get some food in you and then, Jill Tinsley, I want to know all about you."

She laughed. "That will take about five minutes. There isn't much to tell."

"We'll see."

The restaurant was small and cozy and Jill and Chip were seated immediately in a corner booth. They ordered breakfast and sipped cups of steaming coffee while they waited.

"Jill," Chip said, looking at her steadily, "what were you doing walking around that neighborhood alone?"

"Putting flyers on windshields of cars."

"What? Why?"

"To earn extra money."

"It's dangerous down there! Don't you read the newspapers? There are muggings, rapes, all kinds of—"

"I know." She laughed merrily. "I live in that neighborhood."

"You what?" Chip roared, then glanced around quickly and received frowns from people in the other booths. "You live in one of those tenements?"

"Yep. I have my own bathroom so it's not so bad. I

fixed my room up as best I could. It's really quite cheerful."

"But why? I mean, you're pretty, bright. What do you do for a living?"

"Paint."

"You're an artist?"

"No, a house painter. I paint houses, inside and out."

"I can't believe this," he said, shaking his head. "You're hardly bigger than a whisper and you're a house painter?"

"My size has nothing to do with my ability, Mr. Chandler. However, your attitude is very common and I have a great deal of difficulty being taken seriously. It's narrow-minded people like you who are causing me to have an economic setback right now."

"I'm sorry, Jill," Chip said, reaching across the table and covering her hand with his. "You just took me by surprise, that's all." Lord, he thought, her hand was so small and fragile. She lugged around buckets of paint?

What a strong hand Chip had, Jill thought, and so warm. Strength tempered with gentleness.

"Jill, I'm really sorry if I made you angry."

"That's okay." She sighed. "You'd think I'd be used to it by now. No one believes I can do a competent job, just because I'm not built like an Amazon. There are many forms of prejudice, you know."

"I know. Here's our food. Eat up, Jill."

She had to remember her manners, Jill told herself firmly. It smelled heavenly, but she'd take proper little bites and pat her lips with her napkin. Eggs, bacon, biscuits, hash browns. Fantastic.

She smiled at Chip, then began to eat slowly. For the next few minutes she completely forgot that Chip Chandler was sitting across from her as she devoured everything on her plate, the speed of consumption increasing with every bite. When her plate was empty she stared at it a moment, then looked up to find Chip smiling at her.

"Sorry about that," she mumbled. "I ate like a pig. I didn't mean to embarrass you."

"You didn't. Here, finish off these biscuits. The pancakes I have will fill me up."

"Are you sure?"

"Absolutely."

"Talked me into it," she said, lathering a flaky biscuit with butter.

"How's everything here?" the waitress asked.

"We'd like some more biscuits, please," Chip said. "Oh, and an order of those little sausages to go. Just put them in a doggie bag for our cat."

"Doggie bag for a cat. Got it," the girl said, walking away.

"I can't possibly eat more biscuits," Jill said.

"Take them with you in a napkin. Jill, why are you a house painter?"

"Because I enjoy it, I'm good at it, and I'm following in my father's footsteps."

"Your father?"

"My mother died when I was seven, so Dad raised me by himself. He was a house painter and, during the summers when I was off school, he took me along so I wouldn't be alone. He taught me everything about the trade and as I grew older we became partners. We were a great team."

"Were? Where is he now?"

"He died last year of a heart attack."

"Oh, I'm so sorry. You must miss him terribly."

"Yes, I do," she said softly.

"Do you have other relatives?"

"Nope, I'm alone. Well, that's not true. Now I have Cataledge."

"How old are you, Jill?"

"Twenty-three last month, and please don't say I look younger because I've heard it a million times.

What do you and R.J. do for a living, Chip? You certainly have a plushy office."

"What? Oh, we're investment managers. We started Vestco after we graduated from Michigan State and we're doing all right. Jill, what's going to happen to you?"

"Happen?"

"I mean, cripes, this is terrible. You're living in a rum-dum neighborhood, nearly starving to death . . ."

"Things will pick up," she said, reaching for another biscuit.

"How do you know that?"

"I just do." She shrugged." I have no intention of giving up. I get odd jobs here and there to tide me over."

"Yeah, like flyers on windshields," Chip growled.

"Last month I painted a dear little old lady's kitchen. She didn't have any money so she paid me in canned goods and homemade bread. It was a pretty fair trade-off except I did get tired of canned corn. Is Chip a nickname?"

"Huh? Oh, yeah, I'm William Robert Chandler, Jr. When I was born my father said I was a chip off the old block and I was called Chip from the day I came home from the hospital."

"How sweet. I like it. Do you have brothers and sisters?"

"An older sister, who is married and has three kids."

"How old are you? Twenty-nine? Thirty?"

"Thirty. Jill, have you applied for food stamps or some kind of financial aid?"

"Never. I'm a professional painter and I have no intention of living off charity. I earn my own way just like my father raised me to do."

"Somehow I knew you'd feel that way. Did he leave you anything at all?"

"An old panel truck, some equipment, and a sense of pride. I think that's a very nice legacy."

"And I think you are an incredible woman," Chip said quietly. "I've never met anyone like you before."

"Oh, there are lots of us in my neighborhood, people who are struggling to make a go of it. I'm not exactly unique."

"Yes, you are. You really are."

"Doggie bag for the cat," the waitress said, "and more biscuits. Anything else today?"

"Jill?"

"No, nothing thank you. It was delicious."

"Just the check, please," Chip said.

"Have a nice day, folks," the waitress said.

Chip wrapped the biscuits in a napkin and handed them to Jill, who carefully put them in the pocket of her jacket. With Cataledge's treat in her hand she preceded Chip out of the restaurant after he paid the bill. Back in the car, she set the bag on the floor, saying she'd feed the cat later so there'd be no chance of getting the inside of Chip's lovely car greasy.

"Thank you again," she said. "I contradicted myself, I guess. I said I wouldn't take charity but I certainly didn't hesitate to scramble into your car and be whisked off for a free meal."

"Hey, now wait a minute," he said, maneuvering into the traffic. "That was a luncheon date, except we ate breakfast. It was Jill and Chip enjoying each other's company. I'm the one who should thank you for agreeing to go out with me."

She laughed. "Right, because an ugly guy like you must have a tough time getting women to pay attention to him. Come on, Chip, you and R.J. together must chalk up more conquests than you can keep track of."

Chip frowned. "You like R.J.?"

"Well, I don't exactly know him."

"But you think he's good-looking?"

"Who wouldn't?"

"Oh."

"But so are you. Are you fishing for compliments, Chip?"

"No! I was just trying to find out if you preferred R.J., that's all."

"Preferred him over what? Or whom?"

"Me, dammit!" Chip roared.

"Good heavens," Jill said, jumping in surprise. Even Cataledge opened one eye.

"Sorry," Chip mumbled. What in the hell was the matter with him? he wondered. He was acting like a jealous lover or something. He had more women than he could handle, including dippy Brenda. What difference did it make one way or the other what Jill thought of him? None. He certainly didn't care. Did he?

"Are you going back to your office?" she asked.

"Yeah, I have some work to do."

"You can just let me off there then. I only live a few blocks over."

"No way. I'm taking you home."

"It really isn't necessary."

"I said I'm taking—"

"All right! Why are you so crabby all of a sudden? Do you always shift moods so quickly? You're awfully hard to keep up with."

"I apologize. I'm not usually like this. You shook me up, Jill Tinsley. You're a beautiful, honest, independent woman and I hate like hell dropping you off in this crummy neighborhood. Jill, I'd like to see you again. Do you have a phone?"

"No, and the pay phone in the building has been broken for months. You could . . . write me a letter."

"Cute. I want—"

"Turn left at the next street. It's in the middle of the block on the right."

"Jill, I—"

"No need to park. You can just let me out."

"I'll see you inside, Jill."

"Chip, I wouldn't recommend leaving a nice car like this unattended unless . . . Yes, he's there on the steps."

"Who?"

"Zinger. He'll watch your car if you insist on coming up."

"I do. Who is—Lord, he's a mountain!"

"He's a good friend," Jill said, scooping up Cataledge and the doggie bag as Chip stopped in front of her building. "Hi, Zinger," she said, stepping out of the car. "Look at my pretty cat. Her name is Cataledge. Oh, and this is Chip Chandler."

" 'Lo," Zinger said, in response to Chip's nod. In his fifties, Zinger was a bulky six foot eight, and had an unruly crop of gray hair and a weather-beaten face with a nose that had obviously been broken more than once. He was clad only in faded baggy pants and a threadbare brown sweater, despite the biting cold.

"Zinger," Jill said, "would you keep an eye on Chip's car for a few minutes?"

Zinger nodded. "If you want me to, Jilly. How'd the cat get on the ledge?"

"I don't know."

"How did you figure that out?" Chip asked.

"Cataledge? Cat on a ledge." Zinger shrugged. "Simple. Okay, don't worry none about this flashy car. Anyone touches it, I break their kneecaps."

"Your parole officer wouldn't approve," Jill said. "Just stand there and look fierce."

"Yeah, okay."

"Parole officer?" Chip whispered as he and Jill went up the concrete front steps.

"Armed robbery."

"Was he guilty?"

"Oh my, yes, but he's reformed now."

"Did he ever steal a car?" Chip asked, looking worried as he glanced back over his shoulder.

"Don't worry about it, you can trust him. I usually jog up the stairs to keep in shape but I don't think I should jiggle Cataledge that much. We'll take it slow and then you can read the graffiti on the walls. There are some great, profound messages. Ignore the nasty stuff."

"What floor do you live on?"

"Fourth. The penthouse, you understand."

"Of course."

The stairs were narrow, rickety, and so poorly lighted it was difficult to see. After reading a few of the scrawlings on the wall, his eyes wide with shock, Chip decided to ignore the interior decorating. Radios and televisions blared from behind closed doors. Babies cried and women hollered, and there was a strange odor permeating the air. The frown on Chip's face deepened as he and Jill climbed farther up. He glanced at her often, and she was serenely stroking Cataledge's head.

She shouldn't be here, he thought. It was wrong. She deserved better than this. Why did she have to be so stubborn about being a house painter? She could get out of this dump if she'd take another type of job that paid a steady weekly salary. Hell, it was her own fault she was here. But still . . .

"Home sweet home," Jill said, reaching in the pocket of her jeans for her key. "Welcome to my abode, Chip."

He stepped into the room, moving aside just enough to allow Jill to close the door as his gaze swept over the area. It was small but spotlessly clean, the walls papered with yellow daisies and rosebuds. A tattered sofa was partially covered by a bright yellow afghan, and a braided rug concealed some of the chipped tile on the floor. The window overlooked the street, and Chip resisted the urge to look out and check on his car. The kitchen against the far wall consisted of minuscule appliances that were dented in spots. A small table and chairs, an overstuffed armchair, and various painting supplies, including an old wooden ladder, completed the decor.

"Not bad," Chip said. "You've done a nice job in here."

"Well, I papered the walls with scraps I had left over from a job. Mrs. Rosengren down the hall showed me how to make that rag rug on the floor and Zinger taught me to knit the afghan."

"Zinger knits?"

"He learned while he was in jail. Down you go, Cataledge. I hope you like it here. Thank you for escorting me home, Chip."

"May I see you again?"

"Why?"

"I told you. You're a beautiful, incredibly honest woman and I'd like the chance to get to know you better."

"I'm not sure that's a good idea," Jill said, taking off her jacket and placing it on the chair.

"Why not?"

"We really don't have anything in common. Besides, you're too tall. I get a crick in my neck talking to you."

He laughed. "If that's all you can come up with, then I'd say we don't have a problem here. I'll be in touch."

"Well, I don't . . ."

"Bye for now," he said. He cupped her face in his large hands and lowered his head to claim her mouth in a soft, fleeting kiss. "Damn," he growled, and gathered her into a tight embrace. His questing tongue parted her lips and delved into the sweet darkness within.

Jill melted against him, standing on tiptoe to return the kiss with an abandonment that both shocked and pleased her. A tingling sensation started somewhere deep within her and crept through her insistently as the kiss intensified.

"I'll see you soon," Chip said, his mouth still close to hers.

"Yes," was all she managed to say.

She stood statue-still as he turned and left the room, closing the door quietly behind him. She rested her fingertips on her throbbing lips, as if she could still feel Chip's mouth on hers. Shaking her head to snap herself out of her trance, she walked to the window and peered out, keeping out of view.

Chip emerged from the building and spoke to Zinger, then handed him what looked to be a folded dollar bill. The conversation continued and Jill frowned when she saw Chip look back at the building and Zinger nod his head several times. The two men shook hands, then Chip got into his car and drove away.

Yanking up the window, Jill leaned halfway out. "Zinger!" she yelled.

"Yo!"

"Come up here a minute."

"Yeah!"

She opened her door and crossed her arms over her full breasts, tapping her foot impatiently as she heard the stairs creak and groan under Zinger's weight.

"Okay," she said when he lumbered into the room. "What was that all about?"

"I think your cat's pregnant."

"I know she is. Zinger, what were you and Chip talking about?"

"Nice fella. Gave me a twenty for watchin' his car."

"And?"

"He said I should keep an eye out, make sure nothin' happens to you. I told him I do that anyway and he said he was glad I was around. You gonna see him again, Jilly?"

"I—I don't know. It would be so foolish."

"Why?"

"Oh, Zinger, he's from another world. Did you see his jacket? I could pay three months' rent with what it cost. And the car? His office is over by the Renaissance Center. It's so plush and luxurious."

"So?"

"So, he's out of my league. Sit down. I'm going to topple over trying to talk to you. Want a biscuit? They're really good."

"No thanks. You save 'em for your dinner. So Chandler has bucks, big deal. You're as good as any of them society dames he probably takes out. You're better, in fact, because you don't phony up. Did he say he was coming back?"

"Yes."

"Then he will. He looked me right in the eyes when he was talkin' to me. He's an honest man, Jilly. I'll watch his car whenever he comes and I won't take his money no more, seeing how he's your fella."

"He is *not* mine!"

Zinger laughed heartily. "We'll see, silly Jilly. I'm going back outside. Sure do like that cat. When are them babies due? Suppose I could have one?"

"Sure you can, whenever they get here."

"Really? Hey, that's great. I'm goin' down by the river and see what's being peddled. Maybe I can get us some fruit or somethin'. See ya."

After Zinger left Jill scooped up Cataledge and sank onto the sofa. As she shut her eyes, the image of Chip Chandler danced before her. She could see his flashing smile and hear his rich, throaty laughter. The tingling started anew within her as she recalled the feel of his lips on hers, the warmth of his large hands, which had cupped her face so gently.

"Oh, Cataledge," she whispered, "Chip is so, so beautiful. And he's warm and caring. But Zinger is wrong. Chip isn't mine and he never will be. Never."

*   *   *

Chip Chandler stood staring out his office window, his hands shoved into the back pockets of his jeans and a deep scowl on his face.

Jill Tinsley, he thought. Jill, with the great big green eyes and thick dark braids. How would her hair look loose, spread out over a pillow, as she reached up to welcome him into her bed?

"Damn," he said as a shaft of desire shot across his loins. "She's not *that* terrific. Is she? No! A house painter. Cripes. A house painter who is starving, lives in a hole, hangs out with ex-cons, and worries about mangy cats on ledges."

But, oh man, he thought, when he had kissed her he hadn't wanted to stop. Her lips were so soft and sweet and she had responded wholeheartedly. She was something. But she was also right; they had nothing in common. Well, maybe they did. How would they know unless they found out more about each other? At least Zinger was there to watch over her. He would think about dropping by and seeing her in a week or so. If he had time. Did she have any food for dinner? Yeah, the biscuits. Hell, that wasn't enough! She'd probably feed the biscuits to that damn Cataledge and—

"Enough!" he said. "Get out of my head, Jill. You're getting on my nerves, lady."

Zinger returned to Jill's apartment with a bushel basket of apples, and she gave him a cooking lesson in how to make apple crisp, using the biscuits as a crumbly topping. They consumed hefty portions for their dinner, then Zinger disappeared to sit once again on the front steps in the cold night air. Jill knew that his years in prison had made their mark, and that Zinger hated the confines of his small room in the basement of the tenement.

She opened her sofa bed and made it up with thin but clean sheets and blankets. She showered quickly, donned a long flannel nightgown, and turned down the heat to save on her fuel bill. After unbraiding her hair she brushed it until it glowed in a raven cascade down her back. Picking up a library book she snuggled beneath the blankets to read while Cataledge curled up beside her.

Chip Chandler ran his finger around the collar of his stiff white shirt and frowned. What a boring evening, he thought. Brenda hadn't stopped talking since he'd picked her up and so far hadn't said one intelligent thing. The band was lousy. The food was bland. Had Jill eaten? he wondered suddenly. Now, where in the hell had that come from?

"Darling, isn't the music divine?" Brenda said. "You haven't danced with me all night. Come on, Chip, I want to have some fun."

"I'm really tired, Brenda," he said. "In fact, I think I'm getting the flu. Yes, that's it. I'm sick. I'd better take you home before I contaminate you with my germs."

"Home? It's not even eleven o'clock. You don't look sick."

"Oh, but I feel terrible. Even my bones ache. Listen, there's your old buddy Mel over there and he's all alone. I could speak to him and see if he'd give you a lift later."

"Well, I always did like Mel."

"Great. Come on, let's go talk to him."

"You seem awfully anxious to pawn me off, Chip Chandler."

"Me? Don't be silly. I'm sick, Brenda, very sick.

Oh-h-h, my head hurts. I think I'm going to throw up."

"Not on me, you're not," Brenda said, hurrying in Mel's direction.

Just before midnight, Jill closed the thick novel with a satisfied nod at the happy ending and stretched leisurely. A sudden knock at her door brought her scrambling to her knees on the bed.

"Who is it?" she called.

"Jill? It's Chip."

"Chip?"

"Jill, please open the door. I've got to talk to you!"

Two

Jill hurried to the door and slid off the chain, opening the door only far enough to peer out with one eye.

"Chip? What are—"

"Jill, do you know that Zinger is sitting out there on the steps at this hour?" Chip yelled.

"Shhh. Yes, he always does that. He doesn't like being cooped up in his room. But what—"

"He doesn't even have a coat on!"

"Shhh. He used to live in Alaska and says this weather is only a bit nippy. Chip, what are you doing here?"

"Oh. May I come in?"

"Now?"

"I have to talk to you."

"Well, I guess so," she said, stepping back and opening the door.

Chip entered the room and tossed his overcoat onto the overstuffed chair before turning to face Jill. He opened his mouth, shut it, then opened it again. "I knew it," he said. "I just knew it."

"I beg your pardon?"

"Your hair is absolutely fantastic, like an ebony waterfall. You have the most beautiful hair I have ever seen."

"I do?"

"Oh my, yes," Chip said, moving closer and gathering the heavy tresses in his hands. "It's so silky, so lovely."

"Thank you," she said, hardly breathing. Her heart was racing and she seemed unable to tear her gaze from Chip's. For eons or seconds they simply stood there, mesmerized. Jill blinked once slowly as if to see if Chip were a figment of her imagination, but he remained standing before her, smiling with a warmth that matched the glow in his eyes.

"Chip," she said, snapping back to reality, "why are you here dressed like you just stepped off the top of a wedding cake?"

"Huh?" he said, shaking his head to clear the foggy sensation surrounding him. "Oh, my clothes. Ridiculous, don't you think? I prefer jeans. It's freezing in here, Jill. What happened to your heat?"

"I turned it down. Could you explain your visit? My feet are turning blue."

"Then get back in bed!"

"With you here? I don't entertain men in my bed!"

"You get *in*, and I'll sit *on*. That's perfectly acceptable social behavior."

"I don't know about this," she said, hurrying into the bed, covering her pulled-up knees, and wrapping her arms around them.

Chip sat down next to her and tugged his bow tie loose, stuffed it into his pocket, and undid the top button on his shirt. Jill watched him wide-eyed, drinking in the width of his shoulders, the sheen to his thick hair, catching the aroma of his musky aftershave. She clasped her hands even more tightly and resisted the urge to brush back a lock of hair that had tumbled onto his tanned forehead.

Oh, good heavens, he was so beautiful, she thought. He *did* look like a statue from a wedding cake. But . . . "Why are you here?" she asked again.

"I—um—want to talk to you."

"I gathered that. Where were you, dressed like that?"

"At a charity ball. Jill, I—"

"Was it fancy? Well, of course it was. Did they have a band?"

"Yeah, but it was lousy. I—"

"What did she wear?"

"She who?"

"The woman you were with. Did she have on an elegant gown?"

"I don't know." He shrugged. "It was black and clingy."

"Satin?"

"I guess so."

"Were there chandeliers hanging from the ceiling and uniformed waiters and all that stuff?"

"Yeah."

"It sounds wonderful," she said wistfully.

"It was boring as hell."

"I have this fantasy about going to a party like that. My dress will be yellow chiffon. Layers and layers of yellow chiffon with sheer long sleeves and matching shoes. I'll wear my hair all piled on the top of my head and I'll look taller and very sophisticated. The first dance is for me and my escort, just the two of us. There we are, all alone on the floor, and everyone is whispering about what a handsome couple we make. The dashing man and the woman in the pretty yellow dress. Then—Oh, I'm sorry. I'm babbling."

"Your eyes are sparkling," Chip said quietly. "You'll have your fantasy someday, Jill. Yellow dress and everything."

"Not likely. Tell me more about the party. Were all the men dressed like you? Did the women have the most gorgeous gowns in the world?"

"Yes, everyone was decked out in their best. There was a champagne fountain and crystal glasses. The waiters wore white gloves and carried silver trays. One whole wall was a buffet of food, with an ice sculpture in the center of the table. Lots of food. Tons of it. By the way, what did you have for dinner?"

"Me?"

"Yes, Jill, you."

"Zinger bought some apples down by the river and we made a huge apple crisp. I used the biscuits to make the topping."

"Thank heavens," Chip mumbled. "She ate."

"Pardon me?"

"Nothing."

"Would you like some apple crisp?"

"No thank you."

"Cataledge really enjoyed her sausages too."

"Good."

"Thank you for telling me about the party, Chip, but why are you here?"

"Why am I here. Why am I here? Yes. Well. You certainly have the right to ask that, don't you? Um . . . I'm here because—because I want you to paint my living room! Yes," he said, smacking his knee with his hand, "that's it. That's why I came."

"You arrive on my doorstep at midnight looking like a descendant of a penguin to hire me to paint your living room?" she said skeptically.

"Yep." He nodded, appearing very pleased with himself. Nice move, he thought. He wasn't about to tell her he'd come charging in there to find out what she'd had for dinner. He would sound like an idiot! This was smooth. Very smooth.

"Bull."

"It's true! My living room is very dull and drab. It

depresses me and may push me into an early midlife crisis. It has to be brightened up before I slip over the edge."

Jill frowned. "It's too late. The last of the sand just sifted out of your bucket."

"Take pity on me, Jill. I can't bear the thought of another evening in that gloom-and-doom room."

"Gloom-and-doom room?" she said, bursting into laughter. "That's very poetic."

"Will you do it?"

"Well . . ."

"Please?"

"All right."

"Great." He let out a breath of relief. "I'll pick you up about eleven and we'll go to my place so you can check it out. Then we'll have lunch and get the supplies you'll need. Deal?"

"That's reasonable, I guess. Providing I get some sleep in the meantime."

"Yeah, I'd better get out of here," Chip said. Damn, he thought, he really didn't want to leave.

"It is rather late," Jill said. Oh, why had she mentioned the time? she thought. Now he would go and she wanted him to stay a while longer.

"It's too cold in here, Jill. You're going to get sick."

"I spend the whole evening under the blankets. I'm very comfortable. Are you sure you wouldn't like some apple crisp?"

"No, you have it for breakfast. Cataledge is doing okay?"

"Yes, and Zinger is going to take one of the kittens when she has them. Would you like one?"

"I don't think so. Cats don't like me much."

"If you loved it, it would."

"Loving someone doesn't guarantee you'll be loved in return, Jill."

"Maybe not," she said softly. "Have you ever been in love?"

"Not that I know of. If I was, I missed the signals or something. Have you?"

"No."

"You're a beautiful woman. It's hard to believe there hasn't been a special man who . . . Well, it's none of my business. Of course, you could tell me if you wanted to," he added, grinning.

"I've never had time for anything like that. I worked very hard with my father, and after he died . . . No, there's been no one. I guess there have been lots of women in your life."

"Some. Well, more than some, but no one important."

"You just sleep around?"

"Lord, Jill, what a way to put it! I'm discriminate in my . . ."

"Affairs?"

"Yes. No! Why are we discussing my sex life?"

She shrugged. "You brought it up. Are you a good lover?"

"What?"

"Just thought I'd ask."

"Well, I've never had any complaints."

"I didn't think you had. You really have a magnificent body."

"Jill," Chip said, wiping a line of perspiration off his brow with his thumb. "You shouldn't say things like that."

"Why not? It's true."

"It shakes up my libido."

"Really?" She smiled. "Sorry about that."

"Say, is Zinger going to come zooming in here and break my kneecaps if I stay too long?"

"No, he likes you because you looked him right in the eyes when you talked to him. He says you're an honest man."

"I'll be damned," Chip said, smiling. "Did you know

he said he wouldn't accept my money anymore for watching my car?"

"Yes, he told me."

"Well, I guess I'd better be going. Jill, I want to kiss you goodnight. I know you're a little uncomfortable about being in your nightgown and I don't want to blow it. So, if you'd rather I didn't . . ."

"Having you kiss me sounds very nice."

"Oh. Well. Then I will."

He leaned forward and fleetingly brushed her lips with his. In the next instant he shifted closer, gathering her to his chest, and she wrapped her arms around his neck, inching her fingers into his thick hair. Lips parted, tongues met, and their breathing became raspy as the kiss intensified and went on and on. Chip slid his hands to the sides of Jill's full breasts. He cupped the sweet weight in his palms, trailing his thumbs over the nipples, which grew taut beneath the flannel nightgown.

Desire stared to glow deep within Jill, then spread like a flash flame throughout her, bringing a soft moan from her throat. New, strange sensations swirled unchecked from the tips of her toes to her flushed cheeks as she passionately returned Chip's kiss.

His hands moved to her back to press her tightly against the hard wall of his chest, crushing her breasts with pleasant pain. Time, reason, reality held no meaning for Jill as she was swept away by the touch, the aroma, the very essence of Chip Chandler. As they continued to kiss with mounting excitement, she was awash with desires never before experienced. She became acutely aware of her own femininity and rejoiced in it. Where she was soft and gently rounded, Chip was rugged and sharp. How lovely the contrast, how exquisitely they molded together.

"Oh, Jill," Chip said, taking a ragged breath, "I have never, *ever* desired a woman the way I do you.

No, don't say a word because I know I can't have you yet. Kissing you, holding you, is enough . . . for now. Good night, lovely Jill. Sleep well and dream of pretty yellow dresses."

"Good night, Chip," she whispered.

He stood and picked up his coat off the chair. Walking to the door he turned and looked at Jill for a long moment before leaving the apartment. Jill drew a shaking breath and pressed her hands to her warm cheeks. On trembling legs she hurried across the cold floor to slip the chain into place, then crawled back into bed and shut off the light.

What had she done? she thought, staring up into the darkness. Chip had evoked passions within her she had not known she possessed. She had relished the feel of his lips and hands, had wanted to touch every inch of him and discover the mysteries of his masculinity. And Chip had wanted *her*. What had he said? He couldn't have her *yet*, kissing her was enough *for now*? Dear heaven, did he think she was going to make love with him?

"Of course, he does, stupid," she said aloud. "You practically crawled inside his shirt!" She'd led him on, she thought miserably. She was a tease. No she wasn't. Oh yes she was! Chip was used to worldly women in black satin dresses who knew how to play the game. To them, it was a foregone conclusion that sex would be the end of an evening. But for Jill? No. No way. She would have to love and be loved in return before she could give of herself. For with the surrender of her body would go her heart and mind and soul, forever.

"Oh, Cataledge," Jill said, stroking the sleeping cat, "why can't I just live for the moment like other women? Why do I have to have hopes and fantasies? Chip will never love me, and I'll never have a pretty yellow dress. So I mustn't, *mustn't*, fall in love with him. I can't allow it to happen."

With a sigh, she burrowed deeper under the blankets and soon fell asleep. Her dreams were filled with Chip. He reached out his arms and led her across a shining dance floor. They were floating in time to the music, suspended on a billowy cloud of yellow chiffon.

Miles away, Chip poured himself a generous serving of Scotch and downed it in two swallows. He slammed the glass back onto the kitchen counter and shook his head as he began to pace the floor.

He had actually done it, he thought. He'd driven like a lunatic halfway across town to make sure Jill Tinsley had eaten dinner. He was crazy! He really was! And then to cap off his brilliant performance, he'd hired her to paint his living room so she wouldn't figure out why he had shown up in the first place. What an idiot. His living room didn't need painting! He'd had the whole house decorated when he'd bought it six months earlier.

"Dementia at thirty," he said to the ceiling. "Why me, I ask you?" But, he thought, Jill Tinsley was something. She felt like heaven itself in his arms and her lips were ambrosia. She was a virgin, he was sure of it from the things she had said, the wondrous expression on her face after they'd kissed. A virgin, for cripe's sake. He didn't need that kind of situation, didn't want the responsibility of being the first for her. But he ached inside for her, desired her more than any woman he had ever known.

"Stay away from her, Chandler," he said to the cupboard door. "She's trouble, big trouble. Have her paint the damn walls and that's it. *And*, big shot, quit kissing her!"

When Chip finally fell asleep he had a ridiculous dream about cats and penguins dressed in yellow chiffon.

The next morning Jill donned jeans and a green sweater, then braided her hair in a single plait down her back. She gave herself a firm lecture about her dealings with Chip Chandler being strictly business. While she finished the apple crisp, she mumbled on about her role as the house painter and Chip's as the client. There would be no more kissing and touching and warm gazes. She then proceeded to stare at the clock, willing it to move faster, to reach eleven o'clock and bring Chip Chandler to her. She sprang instantly to her feet when she heard the knock on her door, and was smiling when she greeted Chip.

"Good morning," he said, stepping into the room. "Did you have breakfast?"

"Apple crisp," she said. No more kisses? she thought. Oh, how grim.

"Apples are healthy food," he said. Oh, man, he thought. He had to kiss her! Just once. Nothing wild. A little peck. He'd go crazy if he didn't hold her. "Come here, sweet Jill," he said softly, opening his arms to her.

She went. As naturally as breathing she moved into his embrace to be enveloped by his warmth and strength. Standing on her tiptoes she savored the feel of his soft, sensuous lips, joined him in a duel of tongues, and was trembling when he finally released her.

"I didn't intend to do that," he said, his voice raspy.

"Neither did I," she said, convinced he could hear the loud beating of her heart.

"I like kissing you, Jill. No, that doesn't sound right. I like ice cream cones, too, but kissing you is on a totally different plane from ice cream cones. You are very special, Jill Tinsley, and you're doing strange things to my head. We won't discuss what you do to my body. Do you know that I got into my car to come over here and realized it was only nine o'clock and I had to go back in the house? That is not the behavior of a man who is operating on all eight cylinders, kid. Now, however, having kissed you, I feel much better."

She smiled sweetly, "I'm glad. I feel rather nice myself. When you kiss me, it's as though you really mean it, as if at that moment I'm the most important thing in the world for you. You create a private place for us when you hold me and kiss me, and I've never been anywhere like that before."

"Man," Chip said. He shoved his hands into the pockets of his jacket as he walked over to the window, and he stared down at the street below.

"Chip?" Jill said, hardly above a whisper.

"Never in my life," he said, turning to face her, "has a woman said anything like that to me. There are times when I feel like a piece of beef on the hoof, graded on my ability to perform in bed. You're expressing such reverence, placing such importance on my simply holding you and kissing you, and that is incredibly beautiful. Thank you. Thank you more than I can ever say."

Neither moved or hardly breathed. Their eyes met and held as a strange tension built within the small room. Jill felt an amalgam of emotions, not knowing whether to laugh or cry. Had minutes passed or merely seconds? She didn't know as she was held immobile by Chip's mesmerizing gaze.

Suddenly he cleared his throat roughly. "We'd better go," he said, making a pretense of buttoning his jacket, which was already buttoned. "Do you want to bring Cataledge along?"

"I think I'll ask Zinger to watch her. She needs some fresh air."

"Whatever," Chip said, running his hand over the back of his neck.

"What's wrong, Chip? You have such an awful frown on your face now. I'm sorry if I upset you in some way, but I don't know how to be anything but honest with you. I realize you're used to sophisticated women, but that's not who I am. Maybe I should go ahead and say this. I have never before felt the things I do when you kiss me. It's as though my femininity is waking up from a lifelong slumber. But, Chip, I'm not going to make love with you. If I've led you to believe that I'm willing to do that, I apologize."

"I see," he said quietly.

"Do you still want me to paint your living room?"

"Of course! One has nothing to do with the other."

"I think it would be best if you didn't kiss me anymore."

"Why the hell not? Dammit, Jill, give me a break."

"Don't yell! You're the one with the libido that goes off the Richter scale. I'm just trying to do the sensible thing."

"Sensible? Not kissing you is sensible? It's stupid, that's what it is. I want to kiss you. I adore kissing you. I'll kiss you anytime I damn well please!"

"Oh, is that so?" she snapped, planting her hands on her hips. "I might have something to say about that, Mr. Chandler."

"Okay, Miss Honesty, Truth, and the American Way, can you stand there and say you don't want me to kiss you anymore?"

"Um . . ."

"Well?"

"No, I can't say that, but—"

"Fine. That's settled then. Let's go."

"But—"

"Jill!"

"You're a bully sometimes, do you know that?" she said, grabbing her jacket and stomping to the door.

"Yeah, but I'm cute," he said, grinning at her. "You forgot the cat."

Zinger was delighted to baby-sit Cataledge, and, he said, no one had touched Chip's car while Chip had been inside.

"Who would dare?" Chip said to Jill as he turned

the key in the ignition. "A guy with a penchant toward suicide maybe. R.J. and I played football at Michigan State, but I swear there was no one on that team built like Zinger. I bet nobody messed with him in prison."

"Nope. He was very lonely though. Where do you live?" Jill asked as he turned onto Jefferson Avenue.

"Westland. I bought the house as an investment, but I'm getting attached to it and just might keep it. I'm starting to prefer it over apartment living. I have a cleaning lady come in once a week and flick the dust around. It'll be a sharp place once you fix the living-room walls."

"The gloom-and-doom room," Jill said, laughing.

"That's the one, my sweet. Jill, I'm really sorry I switched moods on you so fast back at your apartment. The thought of not kissing you anymore threw me though. As for not making love . . . Well, I can handle that. I think. Sure I can. I'm not a sex maniac, for Pete's sake. I'm simply a normal, healthy man who finds you to be the most desirable—Whew! Tell me to change the subject."

"Change the subject."

"Okay, I will. Jill, why won't you go to bed with me?"

"What?"

"Don't you think I have the right to know? Are you, for example, saving yourself for your wedding night?"

"No."

"But you *are* a virgin."

"Yes."

"So, what's the problem or program or whatever?"

"Love," she said. "I will have to be in love and he, said male person, would have to love me in return."

"Why don't you lower your standards a bit?" he said, grinning. "Settle for good old lust."

"No! Neither rain nor sleet nor—"

"I think that slogan belongs to the pony express or the mailmen."

"Oh. Well, how's this? I shall stand alone and await the one who will meet the needs of my heart and body, and will return such gifts in kind."

"Not bad. Who said that?"

She laughed. "I just did. I made it up."

"You missed your calling. You should have been a poet instead of a house painter. Love, huh? That's a tall order, Jill."

"I know." She sighed.

"May I ask you something?"

"Sure."

"Do you really think I look like a penguin in my tuxedo?"

Jill dissolved in a fit of laughter. The lilting sound danced through the air and was joined by Chip's throaty chuckle. He took her hand and tugged gently, until she slid across the seat and snuggled close to him. He told her tales of his and R.J.'s escapades in college and she laughed in delight. The winter sun waged a battle against the gray sky and won, bringing a glow to the once dreary day. Jill felt young, happy, and carefree, her problems pushed to a dark, dusty corner of her mind.

Chip's home was a two-story brick building on a double-sized lot with a sweeping lawn and tall trees.

"Pretty," Jill said as they walked to the front door.

"It's too big for me, I suppose, but I like it. Enter, madam."

The entryway was tiled and the stairway to the upper rooms sat at the right. Chip led Jill into the living room off to the left and her feet sank into thick brown carpeting. The room was large, the furniture massive, and a fireplace, flanked by glass-enclosed bookcases, took up the center of the far wall. The decorating had been done with a definite masculine flair, but the room was welcoming.

"Oh, Chip," Jill said, "it's absolutely lovely. Wait a minute. The walls are off-white. What's gloomy about off-white?"

"Would you like me to build a fire?"

"That sounds nice. Chip, about the color of the—"

"There's plenty of food here. We could have a picnic in front of the fire."

"Okay. But—"

"Then I'll give you a tour of the place. There are four bedrooms upstairs and a den down here and—"

"Chip!" Jill yelled. "The walls!"

"What about them?"

"There's nothing wrong with them."

"Oh."

"What color do you think you want them?"

"Color? Well, how about . . . white-white instead of off-white. You know, *white*!"

"It'll look like a hospital."

"No, it'll be cheerful and bright. Yes, that's perfect."

She shrugged. "You're the client."

"Let's haul some food out of the refrigerator as soon as I make a fire. We'll go to the store later for paint."

As Chip busied himself preparing the fire, Jill wandered over to one of the glass-enclosed cabinets.

"Owls," she said, smiling, when she saw that several shelves were filled with small figurines. "Oh, Chip, what a marvelous collection. There are so many sizes and shapes, and they're made out of everything imaginable."

"It's a hobby of mine," he said, placing a screen in front of the now roaring fire. "Open the door there. See that one? That owl is hand-carved out of ivory and that one is jade. I have over a hundred of them."

"They're beautiful and so unique. How did you get interested in owls?"

"When I was in fourth grade I had to write a report and for some dumb reason I picked owls. I really got caught up in studying all about them. Did you know that a great horned owl will take on a bald eagle? Anyway, my dad took me up north to the woods and we camped out so I could see the owls at night. Then my mom gave me that little china one there because I got an A on the report. I collected the rest over the years. R.J. thinks it's ridiculous, but he gave me that teakwood one in the corner."

"I think it's a marvelous collection," Jill said. "Your parents sound like very nice people too."

"Top-notch. They retired to Florida last year. My sister lives in Midland because my brother-in-law works for Dow Chemical. I get up north to see them whenever I can. We're a close family, yet we respect each other's privacy too. We're there for one another if anything happens."

"You're very fortunate," she said quietly.

"You're so alone, Jill. Talking about my family made me realize that. It doesn't seem right."

"We can't control things like that. All I can do is accept how things are. My father was good to me when I was growing up and he taught me how to look after myself."

"Don't you get lonely?"

"Sometimes. Zinger and I spent Christmas Day together. It was nice. We even sang Christmas carols until the neighbors banged on the wall. I knitted him an afghan and he gave me a sugar angel."

"Oh, Jill," Chip said, pulling her into his arms, "how can you be so damn brave?"

"I'm a realist," she said, looking up at him, "I know who I am and what I'm capable of doing. I indulge in an occasional fantasy, but most of the time I have my head on straight."

"Fantasies about a pretty yellow dress?"

"Yes." She laughed. "That's one of my best. I have every detail in my mind. You would not believe how gorgeous I am in that yellow chiffon dress."

"Oh yes I would. You'd make Cinderella look like a hag."

"Oh, at least," she said, smiling. "I really enjoyed seeing your owls. Thank you for sharing them with me."

"How about sharing some lunch now? That's after we share a kiss."

Now *that* was sharing, Jill thought as Chip claimed her mouth in a searing kiss. When he finally lifted his head she immediately missed him, wanted more of his warmth and taste and aroma. Wanted to feel the hard contours of his body pressing against the soft slopes of hers and wanted to savor the desire that was swirling within her.

"Lunch," he said, taking her hand and leading her from the room. "Food. Nourishment. Vitamins and minerals. Protein and—"

"Enough already!"

"Oh."

They made huge sandwiches from a multitude of ingredients Chip pulled out of the refrigerator and ate sitting on the floor in the living room in front of the fire. Dessert was enormous dishes of rocky road ice cream, and Jill moaned as she licked her spoon clean.

"I'm stuffed," she said.

"Good. You need to eat more meals like that."

"Are you saying I'm skinny?"

"No way. Your figure is perfect. But I do worry about you not eating properly."

"I'm very healthy."

"Oh, sure. You fainted all over me, remember?"

"That was a fluke. It's never happened before."

"Dammit, Jill, what am I going to do with you?"

"Do?"

"You're consuming my brain!"

She laughed. "You make me sound like an alien monster."

"This isn't funny!"

"Why are you getting all hyper? Are you doing a mood switch on me again?"

"Yes! No! Hell, I don't know," he said, raking his hand through his hair. "Why can't I get you out of my mind? Why do I worry about you? Why do I miss you ten minutes after I leave you? Huh? Huh? Answer me that!"

"How should I know!"

"And," he bellowed, "why do I desire you more than any woman I've ever known? You are driving me nuts, Jill Tinsley."

"Well, excuse me all to hell," she said, getting to her feet. "It's not my fault. You're rather rude yourself, Chip Chandler. I dreamed about you last night and you had no business following me into my sleep."

"You dreamed about me?" he said, grinning up at her. "What was I doing?"

"We were dancing," she said, flopping back down onto the floor. "On a yellow chiffon cloud. How's that for stupid?"

"I rather like it. Has class. Was I in my penguin suit?"

"I don't remember."

"Was I naked?"

"Shut up!"

"Just thought I'd ask. Want some more ice cream?"

"No."

"Do you know what really scares the hell out of me?" he said quietly.

"No. What?"

"That I'll lose control and seduce you, make love to you when you aren't thinking clearly, and then you'll hate me for having done it. It could happen, Jill. When I kiss you I can feel myself slipping into a foggy place, losing touch with what's right and wrong. And you respond to me more every time I touch you."

"Chip . . ."

"Don't say I shouldn't kiss you anymore because we covered that already. I have to tell you, Jill, I have never been so screwed up in my life. How can such a small person have such an overwhelming effect on me? Forget I said that. You're more of a woman than some tall ones I know. Size is unimportant. It's who you are. Back to my question. What am I going to do with you?"

"Have me paint your living room and then . . . forget you ever met me, I guess."

"No can do. That's impossible. Unless you want me to leave you alone, never see you again . . ."

"Oh, Chip, that sounds just awful!"

"Ain't that the truth? Okay, I'm going to muster up every ounce of self-restraint and willpower I possess. I'll kiss the socks off you and quit. It'll probably be good for my character. Either that or I'll break out in hives. I wonder if that cold-shower bit is an old wives' tale? I'll check it out. Enough heavy talk. Let's go buy some paint."

"This room is going to look like a hospital, Chip."

"Oh, good. Then we'll play doctor together. I got caught doing that when I was six years old and my dad whipped my butt."

"Well, I should hope so," Jill said, getting to her feet. "You rotten little kid."

"Problem is," he said, pushing himself up, "it may be that I turned into a rotten big kid. I've never really tested it out before."

"I think you're a very nice man, Chip."

"I hope I am. You sure you couldn't eat another bowl of ice cream? It's a milk product, you know. Really good for you."

"No!"

"Later then. We'll have a snack. Off we go, my sweet. The paint awaits."

The white paint was purchased along with rollers, brushes, drop cloths, and a sturdy new ladder that

Chip said he needed anyhow. The supplies were stored in his garage, then he announced he was hungry as his head disappeared into the refrigerator. His search produced huge peaches, which they ate sliced into bowls with milk and sprinkled with sugar. Chip relit the fire and they settled onto the sofa, staring into the leaping flames.

"I should be getting home," Jill said finally.

"We haven't had dinner yet. We can go out if you want to."

"I haven't stopped eating all day. I don't have room for any more."

"Later you will. It's going to take several days to paint this room, isn't it?"

"Yes. Since I'm just one person working alone, it takes a while. That's why I charge by the job and not the hour. We haven't settled on a price for this yet, you know."

"We'll agree on a figure. I was thinking that it's really a long drive out here from downtown. You'll cut into your profits paying for gas for your truck. So, how's this plan? You stay here during the time you're working."

"I beg your pardon?"

"There are plenty of bedrooms upstairs. I'm not suggesting anything indecent. You can bring Cataledge too."

"I really don't think . . ."

"It makes sense, Jill. I'll be at work and you can paint your little heart out and won't have the long drive twice a day. I'll explain the whole thing to Zinger so he won't break my kneecaps. Well?"

"Spend the nights here? With you?"

"Relatively speaking. You'll be in your bed and I'll be in mine. It'll be like going to camp. Did you ever go to camp?"

"No."

"See? It'll be a great new experience for you. We'll

roast marshmallows over the fire. They always do that at camp."

"Well, I . . . But . . ."

"Say yes."

"Yes."

"Great. Let's go get your clothes and your cat."

"Now?"

"Sure. Then you'll be here and can start painting early tomorrow morning. Right?"

"Um . . . right. I guess. I'll get my coat. It's in the kitchen."

"Okay," Chip said. Holy cripes, he thought, he was a raving maniac! Jill sleeping down the hall from him? Jill, with her hair spread lusciously out over the pillow? He was a masochist, a sick, sick man. But, dammit, now he knew that she'd be warm and safe and stuffed with food for at least as long as she was here. He could handle knowing she was in that soft flannel nightgown that clung to her full breasts and—

"Gear up, Chandler," he said. "Prepare yourself for ice-cold showers."

Dumb, dumb, dumb, Jill thought as she pulled on her jacket. Stay there in Chip's house, sleep in his guest room, picture him in his bed a dozen feet away? Really dumb. Well, it *was* a long drive back and forth. Oh, face it. She adored the idea of being in Chip's home, moving among his things, having him arrive at the end of a work day to greet her as if she belonged there. She would live out one of her fantasies for a few days. There was no harm in that. Was there?

Three

Zinger nodded his approval at Chip's plan and Chip hustled Jill into the tenement before the huge man could think it over any further. Jill packed some clothes in a battered suitcase and carefully added a tissue-wrapped package that she removed from the closet shelf. Cataledge was collected and the trio drove back to Chip's house.

Silence fell between them during the last several miles, and neither Jill nor Chip spoke as they entered his house and removed their coats. Cataledge stretched leisurely and then wandered into the living room to look around.

Jill's mind was playing tug-of-war. She chastised herself for agreeing to stay at Chip's, then in the next instant told herself that it was a logical way to eliminate the long drive to and from the inner city each day. There was nothing wrong with being economical, she decided firmly. It made absolutely no difference that Chip Chandler was rapidly obliterating her sense of reasoning and wreaking havoc with her desires. She would ignore the new and strange stir-rings within her and paint the stupid walls!

Chip hung up their coats in the front closet. He had never been a compulsive man, he thought, had always prided himself on his analytical, organized mind. He thought things through and determined the most effective course of action.

Until now. Since meeting Jill he had been behaving like a nitwit, a dunderhead, a nincompoop. Well, he thought, maybe not a nincompoop, but close. He'd dumped Brenda in the middle of a date to drive across town to check on Jill's menu for dinner. A per-fectly lovely living room was being transformed into a set for *General Hospital*, and then, *then*, he'd pleaded his case like a lawyer to convince Jill to stay at his house. At night. Down the hall. In that damna-ble nightgown that was Victorian as hell, but on Jill looked as alluring as—

"Jill!" he said much too loudly as desire rocketed through him.

"What!" she yelled, jumping in surprise.

"I never gave you a tour of the house. I'll show you to your room."

"Fine."

Carrying her suitcase, Chip led Jill to the first door upstairs and opened it, switching on the light and stepping back for her to enter. She moved just over the threshold and halted, a soft gasp escaping from her lips.

"If you don't like it, there are others to pick from," he said quickly. "When the decorator heard I had nieces she said I should have a very feminine room for them to use when they visit. But if you'd rather use one of—"

"It's lovely," Jill said quietly, slowly walking for-ward. "I have never seen anything so . . . It's as though it were made for a princess."

"It's okay?"

"Oh, Chip, it's beautiful," she said, drinking in the white eyelet-embroidered canopy bed, the dusty blue carpet and curtains, and the gold-trimmed white provincial furniture.

"I'm glad you like it," he said. "I'll leave you to get settled and go down and start a fire. Then we'll have some dinner."

"Yes," she said absently, placing her hand lightly on the frilly bedspread.

Chip smiled at the expression of wonder on Jill's face and quietly set her suitcase on a blue velvet chair. He stood perfectly still for a moment just watching her, but when a lump started to form in his throat he coughed roughly and hurried from the room.

The sudden noise roused Jill from her dreamy state and she shook her head slightly before opening her suitcase. The meager possessions were placed in the drawers and hung in the closet, the tissue-wrapped package carefully laid in the bottom drawer of the dresser. With one last look at the fairyland room, she went downstairs in search of Chip.

She found him in the kitchen dragging food out of the refrigerator, with Cataledge weaving around his ankles.

"How about fancy omelets?" he asked.

"Sounds good. What shall I do to help?"

"You can make a tower of toast," he said, breaking eggs into a bowl. "When it falls over, you know you have enough."

The earlier tension dissipated as they consumed the delicious meal, loaded the dishwasher, and wiped up the counters and table. Chip had made Cataledge her very own omelet, which the cat ate with obvious relish before falling asleep on Chip's foot.

With one last mug of coffee, Jill and Chip settled on the floor in front of the fire in the living room, their backs resting against the sofa. Cataledge leaped onto the sofa and laid her paw on the top of Chip's head.

"Go away, Cataledge," he said.

"She likes you," Jill said, laughing. "Cataledge, be nice to our host. Lie down."

The cat seemed to think about the command, then flopped onto the cushion and began to give herself a bath. Jill turned slightly to look at Cataledge, then set her mug on the hearth and knelt facing the cat.

"Oh, look," she said. "You can see the babies moving inside her. Give me your hand, Chip."

"I don't think so," he said, shifting around to stare at Cataledge's bulging tummy. "She might bite me."

"No she won't. Here." She picked up his hand and placed it on the extended area. "Can you feel them?"

"Man," Chip said, "they're doing the polka in there. That's really something."

"Can you imagine how wonderful it must be when a mother feels her baby move within her? It must be awesome, like living a miracle every day you're pregnant. Knowing you and the man you love have created a new life and it's there, growing inside you, waiting for the moment to be born. Sorry, I'm babbling again. Why are you looking at me like that?"

Oh, good Lord, Chip thought frantically, he was in love with this woman! He, William Robert Chandler, Jr., was in love with Jill Tinsley! That's what had been happening to him, that was the cause of his irrational behavior, and he hadn't even realized what was taking place. He didn't want to be in love! It didn't fit into his program, the game plan he had constructed for his life. How could Jill do this to him?

"Chip?"

"Huh? Oh. Want to roast some marshmallows?"

"No thanks. I'm really full from dinner. Is something wrong?"

"Wrong? What could be wrong? Of course nothing is wrong. Want to play checkers?"

"No, I'd rather just sit here in front of the fire and relax."

"You're tired? Maybe you should go to bed. You know, get a good night's sleep so you'll be full of vim and vigor tomorrow when you paint. A person should always rest before taking on a major—"

"Chip, you're talking a hundred miles an hour! What is the matter with you?"

"Me?"

"You, motor mouth. Do you want to be alone or something? I can go up to my room if—"

"*NO*! Sorry, didn't mean to yell. Just sit here and enjoy the fire."

"Okay." She smiled and leaned her head on his shoulder.

Chip looked to the heavens as if seeking help as he felt the familiar tug of desire in the lower regions of his body. He was a dead man, he thought. He'd never survive this. He had wanted to make love to Jill when he only liked her, but now? He loved her! He was consumed with the thought of taking her in his arms and loving her fully. He would be the first man for her. What a precious gift she would be giving him, and he'd treasure it and her. He'd move slowly and gently, teach her the intricacies of what they would share, watch her blossom like a flower under his touch and kiss.

"You sure you don't want some marshmallows?" he said, wiping some perspiration off his brow.

"No thank you," she said. No, not marshmallows, she thought. That wasn't what she wanted. She wanted only one thing. Chip. In spite of her firm resolve not to fall in love with him, she had gone and done it anyway. As she'd watched the flames flickering shadows over his rugged, handsome face, she'd realized that she loved him completely . . . forever.

"Oh, dear," she said, sighing.

"That sounded very sad," Chip said gently. "What are you thinking about?"

"Stolen moments in worlds that don't mesh."

"Whew. Heavy. Care to explain or are you off in one of your fantasies?"

"Yes," she said softly. "That's where I am. In a fantasy."

"Enjoy," he said, kissing her on the top of the head.

For several minutes they sat in silence, the only sound in the room being the crackling flames and Cataledge's contented purring. Then, as if an unspoken message had passed between them, Jill lifted her head to look up at Chip just as he turned to gaze down at her. In seemingly slow motion, he circled her shoulders with his arm and lowered his head to claim her mouth.

The kiss was so soft, so gentle, that unexpected tears sprang to Jill's eyes. She raised her hand to rest it lightly on Chip's tanned cheek. His tongue sought entry to the sweet inner darkness of her mouth and she parted her lips gladly. Shock waves of desire danced across her senses as the kiss intensified, tongues dueling, mouths moving feverishly, frantically.

Without raising his head, he lifted her into his arms and laid her on the thick carpet, partially covering her body with his as she circled his neck with her arms, urging him closer. His hand slid to the waistband of her sweater, then under it to the soft flesh of her stomach. The feel of his large hand against her sent waves of heat coursing through Jill's body, and her nipples grew taut beneath the filmy lace of her bra.

Chip drew a ragged breath, then trailed kisses all over her face and down her throat. She moved against him, feeling his arousal pressing against her thigh, relishing its announcement of need. Her hands roamed over his back, tracing the corded muscles that trembled beneath her touch. Time, space, reality, and reason were gone. Passions soared and heartbeats quickened as they kissed and caressed each other.

"Oh, Jill," Chip said, his voice strained and raspy. "I—Damn." He pushed himself up and leaned back against the sofa. He drew his knees to his chest and crossed his arms over the tops, resting his head on them as he struggled for control.

Jill rose slowly to her trembling knees and tentatively touched Chip's shoulder.

"No, don't," he said, jerking away. "Don't touch me. Give me a minute, Jill."

"Chip, I—I'm sorry. I . . ."

"I'm the one who's sorry," he said, lifting his head to look at her, a haunting pain flickering through his dark eyes. "I promised you and myself that I wouldn't seduce you, but, oh, damn, Jill, I want you so much. Just go to bed, okay? Go on upstairs. I'm so sorry, babe."

"Chip . . ."

"Please!" he said, a muscle twitching in his jaw. "Go!"

Fighting back her tears, Jill stumbled to her feet and ran from the room, not stopping until she had flung herself across her bed. She buried her face in the pillow and wept, sobs racking her body.

"Oh, Chip," she whispered, rolling over onto her back, "I love you so much. And I know you'll never love me." She shouldn't stay in that house, she thought, but how could she bear to go? All she had was a precious few days to be with him, to hear his laughter, receive his kiss and gentle touch. A short expanse of time to—to what? Give herself to him, make love with the only man she would ever love? But if she did, how would she survive the leaving? Or would the memories be enough to last her the rest of her life? She didn't know what to do. She just didn't.

With slow, heavy movements she changed into her nightgown and crept beneath the blankets on the bed, huddling in a ball like a frightened child left alone in the darkness.

Chip ran his hand over his eyes and down his face as he drew a shuddering breath. He was exhausted, drained. For the first time in his life he was in love and he hated it. He felt naked, vulnerable to an overwhelming emotion that was devouring his mind and body. A tiny whisper of a girl with big green eyes and a cloud of ebony hair had staked a claim on his heart and rendered him defenseless.

He did *not*, he thought fiercely, want to be in love with Jill Tinsley. So how did he stop himself? How did a man regain command of his own life? Hell, he didn't know.

Why had he taken her into his arms, laid her beneath him? His body had seemed to move of its own volition, ignoring the directives of his mind. He had been swept away by uncontrollable passion. What if he had completely lost control and done it? Taken Jill's gift. He'd never have forgiven himself.

Jill asked so little from life, he thought. She wanted only to love and be loved in return. She deserved to have that. Love, and a pretty yellow dress. A closet full of pretty yellow dresses.

"Should I send her away?" he said to the dying fire. "No. Not yet." They'd share the next few days, he decided. He'd be all right because he now understood what had happened to him. Love had caught him unawares, knocked him off kilter, but he had no intention of succumbing to the emotionally depleting state. He controlled his own destiny, his freedom and independence. Love had to be nurtured to survive and he didn't intend to do that. He would ignore his inner feelings for Jill until the flame flickered and died. As quickly as it had encroached upon his sense of reason, he would snuff it out.

How strange, he thought suddenly, to be thirty years old and not know yourself. He had given little thought to love in the past, had neither run from it nor sought it out. Now it had happened to him—and for the first time in his adult life, Chip Chandler was scared to death.

"I can't do it, Jill," he whispered. "I can't give you my soul. I won't love you."

With weary steps, Chip checked the house for the night and climbed the stairs. He stood for a moment outside the closed door to Jill's bedroom, then, with shoulders slumped and head bent, walked slowly down the hall to his own room.

When Jill opened her eyes the next morning she sat bolt upright in bed, having absolutely no idea where she was. Then memory struck her and she sank back against the pillow. Chip. The scene of the previous night flashed before her and she sighed. Bittersweet, she thought.

There were sweet memories of being held in Chip's arms, being kissed and caressed. And then he had shattered the euphoria with his self-incrimination, his disgust at his own actions. She had wanted, tried to tell him he had taken no more than she had offered, but he wouldn't listen, had sent her from the room to deal with his guilt alone. *She* had caused that pain that had radiated from his eyes. *She* had pushed him to his limit of control. Would he send her away this morning? Had he recognized her part, her weight of blame in that disastrous scenario in front of the fire, and would he now declare her unfeeling, a tease?

Unfeeling? She loved him, she thought, as she stood under the shower. Loved him with an intensity beyond description. The desires in her mind to spend every hour in Chip's presence were mingled with the wakening desires of her body to be possessed by him. She glowed under his touch and reveled in his strength.

If only he loved her in return. But that was a fantasy as elusive as the yellow chiffon dress. They were from different worlds, and she would not presume to enter his. He had money, his own company, a luxurious home, and glamorous women. She had nothing to offer him that he didn't already have.

"Oh, double damn," she said, and marched down the stairs.

Chip was standing by the stove when she entered the kitchen and she squared her shoulders before she approached him, deciding that if she didn't cry the minute he looked at her it would be a major victory. He was dressed in dark slacks and tie with a pale blue shirt, his suit coat draped over the back of a chair.

"Beautiful," she murmured, not realizing she had spoken aloud.

"What? Oh, I didn't hear you come in," Chip said, filling two mugs with steaming coffee. "Here, start with this. I want you to fix yourself a big breakfast after I leave, but I have an early appointment and have to hustle. Sit down, Jill. We have to talk."

"You'll be late," she said, sinking into a chair and looking at him with wide eyes.

"Okay, here it is," he said, frowning slightly. "A simple yes or no will do. Do you still want to stay here while you paint like we planned?"

"Yes."

"Good. Do you accept my apology for last night?"

"Yes, but—"

"Good. Will you eat a decent breakfast and lunch?"

"Yes, but—"

"Good. I'll see you tonight." He started to get up from the table.

"Now, you just hold it, bub," Jill yelled, causing Chip to land back on his chair with a solid thud.

"Bub?" he said, his mouth dropping open.

"That's right! Now listen here. I refuse to allow you to take all the responsibility for what happened last night. I was a willing partner in that little endeavor and I enjoyed every minute of it."

"You did?" he said, a wide smile on his face.

"Shut up. The point is, nothing really happened. I mean, you didn't jump on my bones or anything. We are two adults, Chip, and if we decide to indulge in some delectable kissing—"

"Delectable?"

"Are you listening to me?"

"Yes, of course I am."

"I should hope so, because this is important. I see no reason why we can't . . . enjoy each other's company per se, as long as we practice a reasonable amount of . . . restraint. How's that?"

"Sounds good," he said, "but I think I've used up my life's supply of willpower. My next move is probably to tear off your clothes and ravish your body."

"Oh. Isn't that a little extreme?"

"Yep. Could happen though."

"Really?"

"I don't know for sure. It's risky, Jill, very risky. When I hold you in my arms . . . well, all I can think about is how much I want to make love to you, take possession of your body, and make you mine. Something seems to snap and nothing matters but right now, the moment we're sharing. I don't want to hurt you, Jill. I won't take something so rare and special from you and give you nothing. You want—need—to love and be loved in return. I can't offer you that. I just can't."

"At least you're honest," she said quietly.

"Yeah, hooray for me," he growled, getting up and

shrugging into his jacket. "Don't work too hard today. I'll be home by six."

"I'll cook dinner."

"We can go out to eat."

"No, I'd enjoy doing it."

"Whatever," he said, kissing her on the forehead. "Bye, babe."

"Bye," she said, not looking at him.

Oh man, Chip thought as he headed down the hall, how in the hell was he going to stop loving that woman?

Ravish her body? Jill thought, bursting into laughter. My goodness! Well, at least he hadn't thrown her out on her tush. The conversation had gotten rather confusing though. Were they going to do the kissin' bit or not? Ravish her body? Good grief!

After eating the breakfast she had been ordered to consume, Jill straightened up the kitchen and went in search of Cataledge. Cats and open paint cans did not mix, she decided, and Cataledge was put outside to explore the back yard. Jill spread drop cloths over the living-room furniture and floor, then popped the lid on a can of paint. She had begun! The first order of business was the ceiling, and it would be slow going since she'd have to scramble up and down the ladder constantly to move it.

Clad in faded jeans and an old cotton shirt, with her hair braided and tucked under a baseball cap, Jill Tinsley, house painter, was ready to get to work. And, she thought, she was suddenly in a terrific mood.

Chip Chandler was not.

After his early meeting, he paced his office waiting for R.J. to arrive. There was a scowl on his face and his hands were shoved deep into his pockets. A slight noise in the outer office brought him striding out to investigate.

"Oh," he said, "it's only you."

"Well, thanks," the woman said. "Good morning to you too."

"I'm sorry, Helen. I was hoping it was R.J. I've already made the coffee."

"Good for you," she said, tucking her typewriter cover into a desk drawer.

Helen Webb was a cheerful, plump woman in her late fifties who had started working for Chip and R.J. on a part-time basis when Vestco was scarcely more than a dream. She had watched the company grow, and with it its founders. The two men had begun as young college graduates and developed into shrewd and hard-working businessmen. Helen had applauded their courage and drive and had come to love them as a mother. She had struggled with them through the lean times, in the small, dingy office, and would be the first to say they deserved their success. She now worked full-time and had a high-school girl come in twice a week to do the filing. Vestco was flourishing.

"You look as though you've lost your best friend," she said to Chip.

"Impossible," R.J. said, coming into the office. "I'm his best friend and I'm not lost, I'm right here. How's life, y'all?"

"You're late," Chip growled.

"Like hell. You were early."

"Lovely," Helen said. "It's going to be one of *those* days."

"Sorry," Chip muttered.

"Coffee ready?" R.J. asked.

"Yeah, and I'll bring you a cup," Chip said.

"Uh-oh," R.J. said, heading for his office. "He wants something."

Helen laughed and shook her head as Chip followed R.J. with a steaming cup of coffee in his hand. She was continually hoping that her boys, as she referred to them in her mind, would marry and make her a surrogate grandmother of sorts, but neither seemed to have any inclination to settle down and start a family. They were, she often mused, just too darn handsome for their own good and had more women than they knew what to do with. Rotten shame.

"Okay, Chip," R.J. said, sitting down behind his desk, "what's wrong?"

"Nothing," Chip said, flopping into a leather chair.

"Glad to hear that. Then you won't mind if I get to work? Damn, you made this coffee, didn't you? It's awful."

"R.J.?"

"Hmmm?" he said, flipping open a file.

"What would you do if you fell in love?"

"Shoot myself."

"Dammit, R.J., this is serious!"

R.J. leaned back in his chair and studied his friend for a moment before closing the file.

"You're in love?" R.J. asked.

"Yeah, and I have no intention of staying in love. Thing is, I'm not sure how to stop being in love. It's weird, R.J., really weird. I've totally lost control of my mind, my actions. I'm a wreck."

"I can see that. Lord, it's not Brenda, is it?"

"Are you nuts? It's . . . Jill."

"Who?"

"Jill Tinsley, the girl who fainted."

"The one with the mangy cat?"

"Cataledge isn't mangy, she's pregnant."

"But you just met Jill here on Saturday, Chip."

"A lot has happened since then. She knocked me over, R.J. It hit me like a ton of bricks and I fell in love with her. I refuse to be in love, want absolutely nothing to do with it."

"I can relate to that. So, don't see her again. You'll forget about her in time."

"That's a little tough because she's staying at my house."

"What!"

"She's painting the living room."

"Your living room doesn't need painting. Jill's a house painter?"

"Yep, and I hired her to work for me so I could watch over her, and then convinced her to stay at the house while—"

"Your living room doesn't need painting!"

"I know that, but how else was I going to get her out of that tenement? She was starving, freezing to death. Anyway, she's at the house."

"And you're in love with her."

"Yeah," Chip said miserably.

"Not good. Very bad, in fact. On the other hand, she sure was a pretty little thing. There could be certain benefits to having her right there through the cold, long nights."

"I haven't touched her! Well, just a tad, but not like you're thinking."

"Where does she sleep?"

"In that frilly guest room."

"Whew! That's got to be hard on the libido, boy."

"Tell me about it. R.J., how in the hell do I stop loving Jill? You've got to help me here."

"Calm down. You're coming unglued. Okay, let's think this through. You can't ignore her because she's there. You could throw her out."

"Forget it."

"Bad plan. Well, the way I see it, you'll have to go for overexposure."

"Huh?"

"Do a crash course on being in love. Be with Jill, take care of her, follow your instincts, the whole bit. You'll burn yourself out, kill off the love bug, and everything goes back to normal."

"My instincts are to make love to that woman for hours at a stretch."

"So do it."

"It's not that simple. Jill's special. She's never . . . I mean . . ."

"Oh, Lord." R.J. moaned. "She's a virgin. How in the hell—I didn't think there were any left."

"Thanks to guys like us, there practically aren't!" Chip roared.

"I've never laid a glove on a virgin, Chandler! What do you think I am? A louse?"

"Dammit, what am I going to do?"

"I just told you. Go for it. Play hearth and home and bake cookies together. You'll get so sick of this love crap you'll be more than ready to pack Jill off. As for the sex thing, I don't know. That's tough. In all fairness to Jill you shouldn't make any promises while you're working your way through this. It would be kind of rotten to hurt the kid."

"She's not a kid. She's a warm, sweet, honest woman, who—"

"Okay, okay, she's wonderful. So, if she's a woman, she has the right to make choices. If she chooses to have sex with you with no commitment for the future, then that's her responsibility. Let her decide. In the meantime, put the plan in motion. Spend as much time as possible with her doing all sorts of married stuff. You'll be ready to bail out pronto, buddy."

"Think so?"

"Know so. Remember last summer when I took Nicole to the cabin up north for a week?"

"Nicole is a ding-dong."

"True, but that's not the point. I got a real taste of living under the same roof with a woman. It's grim. She had her makeup all over the bathroom, I never had a minute to myself, she did the crossword puzzle before I could get to it. That was my first and last taste of cohabitation. I'm telling you, Chip, this is the answer. Stick like superglue to Jill and you'll have her out of your system so fast you'll probably forget she ever existed. Trust me."

"I'm so desperate, I'll try anything."

"I know you, Chip. You have an overactive conscience. Make sure you don't promise her anything or you'll rake yourself over the coals later. Dump the sex thing right into her lap and leave the decision up to her."

"Okay, I think I have this figured out. Except, what do I do first?"

"Buy her flowers."

"Are you kidding?"

"No, it's so corny it's nauseating, but men in love do that junk. You've got to do all that stuff so you'll realize it's not your cup of tea. You're going to go the whole nine yards and be done with it once and for all. It's a shock cure. You'll hate every minute, so tough up."

"Flowers?"

"Flowers."

"Cripes."

"Love is hell, ol' boy."

"This better work, R.J."

"Guaranteed. I'll be your coach. You've got nothing to worry about."

"Thanks, buddy."

"What are friends for?"

"Flowers," Chip muttered, walking out of R.J.'s office. "I can't believe this."

R.J. laced his fingers behind his head and leaned back in his chair with a smug smile on his face.

"I knew Jill was special the minute I saw her," he said to the ceiling. "This is for your own good, Chipper. He'd better choose me as his best man for the wedding. Damn, he's a lucky son of a gun. He'll thank me for this someday. If he doesn't break my face first."

"Helen," Chip said, "is there a flower shop downtown anywhere?"

"In the lobby of this building, Mr. Observant, and it

doesn't say much for your romantic nature if you've never utilized the facilities."

"I don't have to be romantic." Chip grinned. "I'm sexy."

"Do tell. So, who's the lucky girl?"

"My mother."

"Your mother is allergic to flowers, Chip. Who's the girl?"

"Helen, you can be replaced."

"No, I can't. I'm the only one around here who makes decent coffee. What kind of flowers are you going to get?"

"I don't know. They should be yellow though. She has this thing about yellow."

"Yellow roses." Helen sighed. "They'll cost you a bundle."

"It's a therapeutic expense, cheaper than a nervous breakdown."

"Huh?"

"I'm really lucky to have a friend like R.J., do you know that?"

"I thought we were talking about roses."

"We are. Well, I have work to do. By the way, what color are your living-room walls?"

"Off-white. Why?"

"Not white-white?"

"It would look like a hospital."

"Thanks a helluva lot," Chip said, stalking into his office.

"Helen," R.J. said, coming to her desk, "do you have the file on—"

"R.J., I think Chip needs professional help."

"He has it. Me."

"He's acting very, very strange."

"Fear not, sweet Helen. I have everything under control."

Jill took a break at noon and made herself a sandwich after checking on Cataledge, who was curled up asleep in a patch of sunlight in the back yard. In the freezer, Jill found a small roast and set it on the kitchen counter to defrost. Returning to the living room, she worked steadily until four o'clock, then carried her supplies back into the garage. The ceiling was halfway completed. With the drop cloths removed and the living room back in order, she headed for a hot shower.

Much later, she was dressed in clean jeans and a fluffy pink sweater, her silken black hair flowing down her back. The roast was in the oven, potatoes were peeled, a salad was chilling in the refrigerator, and Jill was having a marvelous time.

"We'll set the table for two," she said to Cataledge, reaching for the silverware. "For Jill and Chip. For Mr. and Mrs. William Robert—No, that's carrying the fantasy too far, Jill Tinsley." But, oh, how she loved Chip Chandler, she thought. How quickly it had happened, and with such depth, such aching intensity. Darn it, though, Chip didn't love her. He had said that morning that he had nothing to offer her. The man wasn't stupid. He knew they came from different worlds and didn't belong together. Actually, *she* had nothing to offer Chip, because he had it all. But for these few days he was hers, and she was going to savor every minute.

"I wonder if he's going to stop kissing me?" she said to a spoon. "I never did figure out how that conversation ended up. And me? What am I going to do if he does? Could I settle for half the pie? Go to bed with a man I love, even though he doesn't love *me*? After all, life is full of compromises. But then again— Cataledge! Get off that table!"

Just before six o'clock, Chip opened the front door and stepped into the quiet entryway.

"Jill?" he called. Yuck, he thought. That paint smelled terrible. "Jill?"

"Hi," she said, coming out of the kitchen. She walked down the hall toward him.

"I—I brought you some flowers," he said, thrusting them at her when she stopped in front of him.

"Yellow roses? Oh, Chip, thank you. I've never . . . Oh, thank you." She buried her face in the soft petals. "I don't know what to say," she said, gazing up at him.

Oh, would you look at her face, Chip thought. What an incredibly beautiful expression. You'd think he'd brought her a diamond necklace. She'd probably never had flowers before. It was so damn corny, but yet . . . "I'm glad you like them," he said, trailing his thumb over her cheek. "You'd better put them in water. I'll go change my clothes."

"All right. Dinner is almost ready. Chip?"

"Yes?"

"You're the nicest man I've ever known."

"Uh . . ."

"I'll meet you in the kitchen," she said, turning and going down the hall.

Chip stared after her until she disappeared into the kitchen, then started slowly up the stairs. Had that gone according to plan? he wondered. If he was supposed to detest this nonsense, why did he feel so warm inside, so damn pleased with himself? That R.J. sure as hell better know what he was doing! He was the nicest man Jill has ever known? Oh, hell!

Four

"Smells better in here than it does in the living room," Chip said, coming into the kitchen.

"Everything is ready so just sit down," Jill said as she drank in the sight of Chip's muscled body in faded jeans and a gray sweater.

"Can I help?"

"Nope. How was your day?"

"Fine. Yours?"

"I got half the ceiling done."

"Don't rush it. I don't want you working too hard. This food looks great."

"Dig in while it's hot."

"Where's Cataledge?"

"Sleeping. She spent the day outside and she's all worn out. How's R.J.?"

Chip frowned. "Why?"

"No reason. I'm just chatting."

"He's okay. Hey, you're a terrific cook."

"Thank you. I had fun doing this. I've never been in

such a fancy kitchen. I think you have every appliance and gadget that was ever invented."

"What kind of place did you have with your father?"

"Just a small house, like a cottage. I fixed it up cute, though."

"Couldn't you have stayed there?"

"The rent was too high."

"Oh. Could you move the flowers over a little? I can hardly see you."

"Sorry."

"Is there anything special you'd like to do tonight, Jill?"

"Do?"

"Yeah, like go bowling, or to a movie, or window shopping?"

"Are we celebrating something?"

"No, I just thought if you wanted . . . My parents go bowling a lot."

"Well, I don't—"

"Or we could watch TV in the den. The living room is too smelly."

"That sounds perfect."

"Okay, TV it is." Yes, he thought, good idea. A quiet evening at home like dull, drab married people. It was definitely going to be boring. Wasn't it?

The meal passed quickly as they talked about a variety of topics. Chip was surprised to learn that Jill followed politics very closely and had a definite opinion on who was doing what. And to his amazement and delight, she knew the names of every player on the Detroit Lions football team. They hotly disputed the attributes of the quarterbacks and she laughed when he told her of his football fumbles at Michigan State.

It was a fun time, a sharing time, and they were both smiling as they finished cleaning the kitchen and headed for the den with a now wide-awake Cataledge in pursuit. The walls of the den were paneled in knotty pine, there was a large sofa and a desk, and thick carpeting. The television was part of a complete home entertainment center and Jill asked for an explanation of what everything was.

"Before we turn on the tube," Chip said finally, "I need to talk to you."

"All right," she said, sitting down on the sofa.

"Would you like me to turn on the stereo?"

"Yes, please."

Soft music lilted through the air, then Chip sat down next to Jill and ran his hand over the back of his neck.

"Jill," he said, "I've been thinking about what happened last night and what you said this morning. You indicated that you rather enjoyed it when we were . . . were . . ."

"Every minute," Jill said cheerfully.

"Well, it occurs to me that I'm not giving you enough credit here. You're an adult, a woman in charge of your own life, and you have the right to change your mind about things if you should so choose."

"You sound like a lawyer. What things?"

"Sex."

"What!"

"Now, don't get excited," he said, raising his hands. "This is going to be a calm, meaningful discussion."

"Oh. Well, carry on then."

"Yes! You are aware that I called a halt to our—to the activities of last evening and that I suffered a helluva lot of guilt."

"Lawyers aren't supposed to swear."

"Dammit, Jill, pay attention!"

"Sorry."

"Where was I?"

"Suffering."

"I did, you know."

"Physically or mentally?"

"Both, and cold showers are worthless. Jill, what I'm trying to say, but can't because you keep interrupting me, is that the reason I stopped . . . doing what I was doing is because of what you said about loving and being loved in return. You do remember saying that?"

"Of course."

"Anyway, I've come to the conclusion that I'm denying you your right to control your own life. I know where I stand. I want you, want to make love to you, and will definitely not change my mind on the subject. You, however, may have second thoughts regarding the matter and wish to reconsider your earlier declaration. If you do, I will proceed with . . . doing what I was doing, only *completely* doing what I was doing, and not feel guilty because it was your decision. Did you get that?"

"Yes."

"Read it back to me."

"If we make love, it will be my fault."

"Oh, man," Chip said, sinking his head into his hands. "Did you have to put it that way?"

"Isn't that what you said?"

"Fault indicates guilt, Jill. It will be by mutual agreement with no regrets."

"And no promises."

"No, no promises," he said quietly. "The whole thing is up to you."

"May I think it over?"

"Of course. Take all the time you need."

"Thank you. In the meantime, are you planning on kissing me?"

"I'm not sure that's a good idea."

"This is borderline blackmail, Chip. You're doing an 'all or nothing' number on me. That's not fair."

"It's not?" He frowned. Dammit, he thought, where was R.J. when he needed him? This wasn't going well at all. If he started kissing Jill and it got out of control, she could still accuse him of seducing her, and he didn't need that trip. But if he didn't kiss her, how would she be able to know if she wanted him to make love to her? What a confusing mess.

"Chip? Did you die?"

"What? Oh, I was thinking. I really don't know quite what to do here. I don't want to make any mistakes."

"This is getting awfully clinical," Jill said, sighing deeply. "I'm waiting for you to jump up and say, 'To do or not to do, that is the question!' "

Chip laughed. "Now that was funny. I think we should give this topic a rest for now. Let's watch TV."

"Oh, wait. This is one of my favorite songs. I've never heard it played without the words before and it's beautiful."

"Yes, it's nice."

The lovely music was the only sound in the room. After a moment, Chip raised his hand and began to stroke Jill's hair, lifting it and letting it slide through his fingers. Shifting slightly he placed one long finger under her chin and turned her face toward his. Their eyes met, held in a timeless gaze, and then at the same moment they moved toward each other, lips touching, parting, tongues meeting.

As Chip gathered Jill close to his chest, she lifted her arms to encircle his neck. The music played on, enveloping them in a private symphony of sound created only for them. Chip slid his arm under Jill's knees and laid her on the sofa, resting on one elbow to keep his upper body from her as he placed one leg over both of hers.

Pausing only to take a ragged breath, he claimed her mouth again feverishly as Jill urged him closer, sinking her fingers into his thick dark hair. His hand moved under the bottom edge of her sweater, inching upward to cup a full breast. The nipple grew taut, straining against the filmy material of her bra, and Jill moaned softly as desire shot through her.

"Let me see you, Jill," Chip murmured, close to her lips. "Please, babe, just let me see you."

She looked into his dark eyes, seeing the warmth, the tenderness, and nodded slightly. She slid her arms from around his neck and held her breath as he drew the sweater over her head and dropped it on the floor. Her bra followed quickly.

"You're beautiful, Jill," he said, his voice raspy. "So beautiful."

"No one has ever said that before. Am I, Chip? Am I really beautiful?"

"Oh, yes. Yes. And I'm the first man to see your breasts, to touch them. Tell me how this feels, Jill. Tell me." He lowered his head to draw one rosy nipple into his mouth as his thumb trailed over the other, bringing it to throbbing awareness.

Jill gasped, her eyes widening for a moment and then drifting closed as unfamiliar yet wonderful sensations swept through her. Hot, searing desire danced and swirled, igniting a flame of passion within her as Chip's mouth found her other breast and gave it the same maddening, tantalizing attention.

"Tell me," he whispered.

"Wonderful," she murmured. "I've never felt so wonderful, so alive . . ."

He leaned back and tugged off his sweater, watching her face as she gazed at the curly mass of hair on his chest, the corded muscles, the fine film of perspiration glistening on his torso.

"Touch me, babe," he said, lifting her hand and placing it over his heart. "That's it. Touch me."

An expression of awe, wonder, of one discovering great mysteries came over Jill's flushed face as she tentatively moved her hands across his firm chest. She tangled her fingers in the moist hair, then looked at him questioningly when she brushed his nipples and he gasped.

"Don't stop," he said, a muscle twitching in his neck. "It's heaven, sweetheart. You have the touch of an angel."

Oh, how was it possible? Jill thought dreamily as her hands continued their languorous journey. How was it possible that she was pleasing this man? But she was; the desire reflected in his eyes said so. And that desire was for her, because of her, and she reveled in the knowledge.

He leaned forward and once again drew the taut bud of her breast into his mouth. Her hands slipped around to his back, and his muscles trembled under her gentle touch. The song on the stereo had ended but neither noticed as labored breathing and soft moans created a rhapsody of their own special music.

Chip suddenly took possession of her mouth in a searing kiss as he shifted her beneath him, covering her with his hard body. He circled her hips with one arm and lifted her to him, his manhood strong and full against her. Jill felt as if she were weightless, floating above time and space, as she arched her back and heard Chip moan deep within his throat.

How she wanted him, she thought frantically. Her body was aching with a sweet pain she'd never known, as the flame of passion grew. A flame only Chip could quell. He had shown her so much, brought her so far, but she wanted more. Much, much more. His masculinity promised greater gifts, yet unknown joys, and she must have it all. There were no more doubts or fears. The time had come.

"Chip," she whispered. "Chip, I—"

"Aaak!" he yelled, stiffening above her and causing her to gasp in surprise.

"Chip, what—"

"Dammit!" he roared. "Cataledge is on my back and she's digging her claws into me. Ow! Stop it, cat!"

"Oh, no," Jill said, peering over Chip's shoulder. "Cataledge, get down."

"Would you get her off me?"

"I can't. She's really hanging on. Chip, move a little so I can wiggle out."

"I'll kill her! I swear, I am going to kill that animal!"

"Oh, dear," Jill said, sliding out from under Chip and landing with a rather solid thud on the floor. "Come on, Cataledge. This is not nice of you. Chip is your friend, remember?"

"Not anymore I'm not!"

"That's a good girl, Cataledge." She extracted the cat and set her on the floor. "No damage done," she said, peering at Chip's back. "The skin isn't broken."

"I can't believe this," Chip said, flopping flat down and burying his face in a throw pillow.

Jill pulled her sweater over her head and stuffed her bra in her pocket, then tentatively tapped one fingertip on Chip's back.

"Hi!" she said brightly.

Suddenly Chip's shoulders began to shake and a strange noise erupted from the pillow.

"Chip?" she said in a small voice, chewing nervously on her lower lip.

"Oh, man," he said, flipping over onto his back as he roared with laughter. "Oh, man, oh, man."

"You're laughing? Why are you laughing? Chip, stop it."

"I—" he began, but dissolved again into laughter.

"Chip Chandler, shut up!"

"It's like a slapstick movie! I mean, who would believe this? I'm with the most beautiful, most desirable, passionate woman I have ever known and a cat—a cat!—"

"Am I?" Jill whispered. "Am I the most beautiful, the most desirable?"

"Oh, yes, babe, you are," Chip said softly, rolling onto his side and looking down at her. "Jill, tell me you're not sorry I touched you like I did. Your breasts are so lovely, and I'll cherish everything we shared. Your hands, too, were sent straight from heaven just for me. Are you sorry, Jill?"

"No. I have never in my life been so glad that I'm a woman. I don't regret any of it. You made me feel . . . I can't even explain it. Chip, there's no doubt in my mind now. You've shown me so much, but I want it all. I want you to make love to me."

He gently cupped her cheek with his hand and gazed at her with the most incredibly tender expression that Jill had ever seen.

"Thank you," he said, his voice strangely husky. "Thank you, Jill Tinsley. I *will* make love to you, but not tonight. We've just created some lovely memories and I want to savor them, relive them in my mind. It was so special. Do you understand?"

"Yes."

"When we come together it will be a celebration. We're going to be fantastic. Soon, my sweet, very soon."

"All right, Chip."

"Ow! Dammit, now Cataledge is attacking my leg! What in the hell is the matter with her? I'm the guy who bought her sausages and cooked her an omelet! I—hoo-boy, I think she's in labor."

"Really?" Jill said, scrambling to her feet.

"Yeah," Chip said, yanking his sweater over his head. "I'll get a box out of the garage. There're towels under the sink in the bathroom down here."

"I'll get one," Jill said, heading for the door. "Oh, this is scary."

Cataledge paced the floor in front of the box that contained a fluffy pink towel. She meowed loudly and arched her back as Jill wrung her hands.

"I think we're making her nervous," Chip said. "Let's leave her alone."

"Oh, Chip, I don't know. She came to you to tell you she was in labor."

"We'll try it. Come out in the hall."

They looked silly, Jill supposed. Two adults peering around a doorway at a pregnant cat. But, darn it, childbirth or kittenbirth or whatever was not to be taken lightly. All kinds of terrible things could go wrong.

"There she goes," Chip said. "Right into the box. We have been dismissed."

"I'm not leaving."

"Yes you are," he said, taking her arm and escorting her down the hall. "We'll have a snack and then you're going to bed. It's getting late."

"You're bossy."

"I like my house painters well-rested and alert so they don't start slopping paint all over."

"But what about Cataledge?"

"I'll keep an eye on her for a while. She's perfectly capable of handling this on her own though. I guess I'm banned to the kitchen. The paint has the living room, the cat has the den. Wonderful."

After drinking some hot chocolate the pair once more peered into the den.

"She's giving herself a bath?" Chip said. "Now?"

"How long does it take to have kittens?"

"Don't look at me, I've never done it. Okay, off to bed with you."

"Aren't you going to kiss me good night?"

"No, because I am very aware, believe me, that you aren't wearing a bra and if I took you in my arms right now . . . Nope, I'm not kissing you."

"Plant a peck right there," Jill said, tapping her forehead.

"That I can handle," he said, doing as he was instructed. "Good night, Jill."

"Good night," she said, starting up the stairs. "Will you wake me when Cataledge has the kittens?"

"No. You can see them in the morning."

"Pooh."

"Jill?"

"Yes?"

"Thanks, babe. I mean that. Tonight was . . . Well, thanks."

"Good night, Chip," she said softly.

A half hour later, Jill gave up the attempt to sleep and switched on the small lamp on the night stand. She drew her knees up and rested her chin on top of them. She had told herself her tossing and turning was due to concern for Cataledge, then admitted she was lying. Her mind was consumed with Chip and what had happened in the den.

He was right, she thought. They *had* created beautiful memories. She would never forget the feel of his hands and mouth on her breasts, or the exquisite splendor of his naked chest and back. What an incredibly sensitive man, to want to cherish what they had shared before going on to when they would become one.

Soon, very soon, he had said, and at the thought, desire danced through Jill. Her breasts grew taut at the memory of Chip's tantalizing touch and she shivered slightly under the onslaught of sensations. She wanted to go to him *now*, give of herself and receive what he had promised. She knew she would never regret giving her body—all of herself—to Chip Chandler. She would settle for half of her dream. That he didn't love her in return wouldn't be allowed to matter. She would wrap herself in her memories when she left him and went back to the world where she belonged. And would probably love Chip forever.

Filled with restless energy, Jill slipped out of bed and took the tissue-wrapped package out of the dresser drawer. She opened it carefully as she settled back against the pillows, brushing her hand gently over her precious treasure. It had been the last gift from her father and she had cried when he had given it to her. He had known what her utmost dream was, the dream she still knew would never be hers. There had never been, never would be, the time or the money for her to reach her elusive star. Her father's gift had said he understood and wished it could have all been different for her.

It was a sketch pad of the finest quality paper and a small set of artist's pencils. During the past year, Jill had chosen her subjects carefully, having only twenty pages in her book on which to draw. The last picture she had done had been of Zinger, and she stared with affection at his rough yet tender face.

There was only one sheet remaining in the pad. With steady, even strokes, Jill began to bring to life the image of her love, of Chip. He was smiling, his eyes radiating that tender, fathomless gaze that melted her heart. His hair was tousled, his neck strong as Jill put the finishing touches on the creation.

"Beautiful," she whispered. "You are so beautiful."

A soft knock at the door brought her upright on the bed.

"Jill? Are you awake?" Chip asked.

"Yes," she said, hurrying to the door and swinging it open.

"Four," he said, grinning at her and holding up as many fingers. "They're beauties."

"I've got to see them," she said, hiking up her nightgown and running down the hall.

Chip started to follow, only to stop when he noticed the sketch pad lying on the bed. Walking over he picked it up, a frown creasing his brow when he found himself staring down at an image of himself, so perfectly drawn he could have been looking in a mirror. He quickly flipped through the pad, his eyes widening at the workmanship, the excellence he saw. Carefully replacing the pad as he had found it, he shook his head slightly in wonder and left the room.

Jill was sitting on the floor crooning to the kittens and praising the new mother on a fine performance. Chip stared at her, realizing he was seeing a part of her for the first time.

She was an artist, he thought incredulously. A brilliant, talented artist! She painted houses when she could be creating such beauty on paper? Why? Hell, that was easy to figure out. She'd worked with her father, been his partner so they could keep a roof over their heads. Now she was scrambling to keep from starving to death. She hadn't had the time to use her God-given gift. She'd been too busy trying to survive. Damn.

"Aren't they darling, Chip?" she said.

"Huh? Oh, yeah, they're really cute," he said. Well, now *he* knew what she was capable of doing and he'd help her achieve her potential. He knew some art dealers who—Hold it, Chandler, he thought suddenly. He was supposed to be falling out of love with this woman, not planning her future. No, it was fine. If he got her started on the right track, he could put her out of his mind. She could move to a decent place and then he wouldn't have to worry about her anymore when she was gone. Gone? Of course. Gone.

"I wonder if they're girls or boys," she said.

"It's too early to tell," he said absently. She had been so trusting, he mused, had responded so willingly and freely. He'd thought he would fall apart when she'd touched him, and then she had said it. She wanted him to make love to her. R.J.'s plan had worked. She had made the decision and his conscience would be clear when they made love. So why hadn't he done it? Because, as unbelievable as it was even to himself, he had meant what he had said. He wanted to cherish the memories of that night, of what he had shared with Jill in that room. He honestly didn't know why, but one thing was certain. He was doing a lousy job of falling out of love with Jill Tinsley.

"Okay, Cinderella," he said, "the party is over. Back to bed."

"Oh . . ."

"You can play mother all day tomorrow. Nice job, Cataledge. You outdid yourself."

Outside Jill's room, Chip shoved his hands into his jeans pockets and looked down at her.

"Do you have other dreams besides pretty yellow dresses?" he asked quietly.

"Oh, sure, but I'm very partial to the yellow-dress scenario."

"I'm serious, Jill."

"Then I guess I don't understand the question."

"Never mind. We'll talk about it another time," he said, kissing her on the forehead. "Bull's-eye. I'm getting good at that. See you in the morning."

"Good night, Chip."

"And go to sleep this time," he called over his shoulder as he walked down the hall.

Jill laughed softly as she went into her room and closed the door. After one last look at the picture she had drawn of Chip, she rewrapped the sketch pad and pencils in the tissue and placed it in the drawer. In bed, she snuggled into the pillow and fell instantly asleep.

Chip, however, lay in the darkness wide awake, his mind waging a battle, causing him to toss and turn. What if he were wrong? he thought, punching his pillow. What if his untrained eye had seen more talent in Jill's drawings than was actually there? He had been so shocked to see his own face smiling up at him that perhaps he'd overreacted. Zinger had looked so alive he could have leaped off the paper and broken

Chip's kneecaps. But what did Chip know? It would take an expert to determine the quality of Jill's work.

"So?" he said aloud. "Now what?" Jill had had enough disappointments in her life, he thought fiercely. How cruel it would be to praise her talent, tell her there was a whole new world open for her out there, only to find it just wasn't true. He couldn't run the risk of having her hurt like that. He had to come up with some way of finding out first.

"I'll sleep on it," he muttered, yawning. "I have to do this right."

The next morning he found Jill sitting in front of the box containing Cataledge and the kittens. Smiling and shaking his head, he hauled a complaining Jill into the kitchen for breakfast, where they prepared scrambled eggs, bacon, and toast.

"Got to run," Chip said, shrugging into his charcoal-gray suit coat. "Don't work too hard, babe."

"I'll get the ceiling finished today."

"Want to go out to dinner to celebrate Cataledge's new family?"

"Well, I . . . No, I . . ."

Damn, Chip thought, she didn't have anything nice to wear. That was why she was hesitating. Where was his brain, for Pete's sake? "I have a busy day planned," he said. "Know what sounds good to me? I'll come home, get out of this suit, and we'll just go out for pizza. Unless you'd rather go someplace fancy . . ."

"Pizza is perfect," Jill said, throwing her arms around his neck. "I adore pizza. I haven't had pizza in ages. I'll gobble up a ton of—"

Chip's lips silenced her chattering with a kiss that brought her melting against him. He gathered her close, his hands roaming over the soft, faded material of her shirt as his tongue explored the secrets of her mouth.

"Must go," he finally said, his mouth close to hers.

"I'll walk you to the door," Jill said shakily.

"No, I—I left some papers in my room that I need. I'll run up and get them. You sit and have another cup of coffee."

"Okay."

Chip grabbed his briefcase and sprinted up the stairs two at a time. In Jill's room he looked around frantically for the sketch pad, yanking open the closet door and then the dresser drawers. When he found the tissue-wrapped package he slipped it into the briefcase, a wave of guilt washing over him.

It was the only way, he thought. He had to protect Jill from any potential pain. He'd quietly investigate her abilities, and if he'd overestimated her talent, she'd never know, wouldn't get her hopes up. It was a good plan but he felt sick to his stomach to be sneaking around, taking her private possessions. But it had to be this way!

"Bye, Jill," he called from the front door.

"Bye," she yelled, poking her head out of the kitchen. "Have a good day."

After she finished her coffee, Jill cleaned up the dishes, visited the kittens, then started work on the living room. She hummed as she went, not realizing it was the song that had been playing on the radio the previous night.

When R.J. sank into the chair opposite Chip's desk, he waited for Chip to stop staring at the ceiling. After several minutes R.J. cleared his throat noisily, and Chip jerked in surprise.

"Don't sneak up on me," Chip growled.

"Right. Well?"

"Well what?"

"How'd it go? The flowers."

"Not so hot."

"Why not? Didn't Jill like them?"

"She loved them. R.J., she was glowing. I mean, you should have seen her face. How could I hate doing something that made her that happy? I felt like a million bucks."

"Oh," R.J. said, suppressing a smile. "Well, not everything is going to work, you know. Different strokes for different folks. Did you have the heavy-duty sex talk?"

"R.J., I think it's pretty adolescent to be sitting around discussing our sexual activities like this was a locker room or something. It's very tacky."

"I understand perfectly," he said, nearly choking on his swallowed laughter. "I won't bring it up again. I guess you didn't fall out of love with her yet, huh?"

"Hell, no! Oh, Cataledge had four kittens."

"That's nice. You can start a pet store. Did you and Jill go out last night?"

"No, she cooked dinner and we stayed home."

"Good thinking. Boring as hell."

"Well, no, it was . . . R.J., I've got a proposal to do for that new client."

"Sure, buddy. Do you need more advice from your coach here?"

"Not today. I have something in the works."

"You're doing great. Just keep up the game plan and you'll be out of love with Jill in no time. Hang in there, Chipper."

"Yeah," Chip said, staring at the ceiling again.

R.J. managed to get back into his office and shut the door before he dissolved in a fit of laughter. "Aw right," he said, punching his fist in the air. "He's a goner. I wonder if he'll name his first son after me? That's after I get out of my body cast."

At eleven o'clock, Chip walked past Helen's desk and out of the office without a word. The secretary shook her head and frowned. When Chip retraced his steps to retrieve his forgotten jacket and overcoat, she eyed him warily and clamped her mouth firmly closed.

"Chip, my boy," the elderly gentleman said, "great to see you. How are your folks? Sure miss those golf games with your father."

"They're fine, Mr. Kellis. They're thoroughly enjoying their new life in Florida."

"Glad to hear it. Another year and I'll be retiring myself. So, what brings you to my humble gallery? I didn't know you were interested in art."

"You have the finest gallery in Detroit, sir, and I need your opinion on some work I've brought with me."

"Fair enough. Let me have a look."

Hesitating a moment, Chip took a deep breath and then handed Jill's sketch pad to Mr. Kellis. The minutes dragged by with agonizing slowness and Chip could read nothing in the expression on Mr. Kellis's face. The gallery owner studied each page carefully before moving on to the next. Chip shifted in his chair and waited.

"Who is the artist?" Mr. Kellis asked finally.

"Her name is Jill Tinsley."

"And no one is representing her?"

"No."

"I want exclusive rights to present her pictures, Chip. A contract bringing in her work on consignment. There are twenty drawings here and I'll need at least a dozen more to have an adequate showing. Unless, of course, you don't want the one of you displayed."

"I beg your pardon?"

"The expression she captured on your face will tell

the world you're looking at someone you're deeply in love with."

"Me?" Chip croaked. "You can tell by—But Jill doesn't even know how I feel about her."

"Well, the drawing speaks volumes, but perhaps she's not realizing what she's seeing. You can decide later if you want to hold that one out. Do we have a deal?"

"You're saying that Jill is really a talented artist?"

"A natural. We'll mat these on black to emphasize the light and dark contrasts. I'm putting together a show for a month from now and I want Jill's work in it. When can she come in to sign a contract?"

"I can't believe it," Chip said, tugging his tie down a few inches. "Mr. Kellis, Jill doesn't even know I'm here. I was trying to protect her from being disappointed if her drawings weren't really any good. I've got to talk to her, explain what I've done."

"I see. Well, I'm sure she'll be pleased, very grateful. You're about to launch her career. When can I expect to hear from you?"

"As soon as possible. I'll talk to her tonight. Thank you, Mr. Kellis. Thank you very much."

"And I thank you. There's nothing more exciting than discovering new talent. I predict Jill Tinsley is going to make a name for herself in the artistic community. Remember, I'll need a dozen more drawings."

"Yes, sure, fine. Thanks again," Chip said, shaking hands with Mr. Kellis after placing the sketch pad in his briefcase.

Chip hardly remembered leaving the gallery and driving back to the office. Jill was an artist! he thought, his mind whirling. That was fantastic, terrific, great. Then why was he so depressed? He wanted her to have this chance. She'd make big bucks . . . and not need him anymore. Not need him for a damn thing. She'd walk out of his life and into a world of money, recognition, sleazeballs who would try to take advantage of her.

"Hell," he said, smacking his palm against the steering wheel. What was the matter with him? Everything was going better than he had even dared hope. Jill would get her life in order and he could regain his emotional equilibrium once she was gone. He'd forget her soon enough, fall out of love with her right on cue. Good. So why was he so depressed?

On an impulse he drove several blocks past the office and parked in front of Jill's tenement. Zinger lumbered to his feet and scowled as Chip got out of the car.

"Why are you here?" Zinger asked. "Has somethin' happened to Jilly?"

"No, she's fine, just fine. Why don't you sit down? I'll join you, okay?"

"Yeah," Zinger said, lowering himself back onto the steps.

"I just thought you'd like to know that Cataledge had four kittens last night," Chip said, sitting down next to the huge man.

"No foolin'?"

"Yep. They're cute little buggers. You can have yours in a few weeks, I guess. Zinger, do you remember when Jill drew that picture of you?"

"Yeah. It scared me sort of. There I was on that there paper, you know what I mean? One of them pictures is of her father. The rest are folks here in the neighborhood."

"Did she mention anything about hoping to become an accomplished artist?"

"No, she didn't say nothing like that, but I seen the look on her face when she was drawin'. She was in a world of her own. I don't think she lets herself dream about it 'cause it means too much to her. She daydreams about pretty yellow dresses instead. Jill knows who she is and she ain't kiddin' herself about ever bein' more than that. It's a lesson we learn real quick-like down here."

"We'll see, Zinger," Chip said solemnly. "We'll see."

"Don't hurt my Jilly, Chandler," Zinger said, and Chip heard the warning in his voice.

The two men sat in silence for several minutes. Finally Chip pushed himself to his feet and without speaking walked to his car and drove away.

Zinger watched Chip's car until it disappeared, then a slow smile crept over his weather-beaten face.

Five

"Jill!" Chip yelled as he came in the front door.

"In the den!"

"Now, does that surprise me?" he said as he joined her. "Nope. How's the gang?"

"Fine," she said, getting to her feet and wrapping her arms around his waist. "And you?"

"Okay. I'll go change and we'll head out of here for some pizza. By the way, I went to see Zinger today to tell him about the kittens."

"You did? As busy as you are you took time out to see him? That was so thoughtful of you, Chip. Thank you. Is Zinger all right?"

"I guess so. Doesn't he ever smile?"

"Not too often. He has a marvelous laugh. It rattles the pictures on the walls."

"Speaking of pictures . . . Um . . . I'll go change my clothes."

"Thank you again for visiting Zinger. I'm glad to know he's doing all right. I miss him."

"You do?"

"He's my closest friend, and he's very important to me. Sometimes we sit on the steps for hours and don't say a word, but he's there. Do you understand?"

"Sure, babe," Chip said, kissing her quickly on the lips. "I'll be right back."

He sprinted up the stairs and stopped at the top, peering down to make certain that Jill had gone back into the den. Hurrying into her room, he pulled the sketch pad from his briefcase and slid it into the bottom drawer of the dresser.

Like a thief in the night, he thought, stalking down the hall to his room. Like a crummy thief in the night. Jill would see why he had done it that way, though. He'd explain it all to her very carefully so she'd understand that he had been protecting her from potential heartbreak. She had a chance at a whole new life and she'd be thrilled out of her mind.

Snow flurries were just beginning as they left the house. A brisk wind was blowing the white flakes into swirling circles and Chip turned on the heater.

"I finished the ceiling today," Jill said. "Since you don't want to sit in there because of the odor, I left the drop cloths in place. Is that okay?"

"Whatever."

"What kind of pizza do you like?"

"Doesn't matter."

"Chip, what's wrong?"

"Nothing. I'm just a little tired."

"We could have stayed home and I'd have cooked dinner."

"No, this is fine. I'll get a second wind as soon as I get something to eat. You worked hard today, Jill. You're not the maid too."

"But I don't mind cooking."

"We're getting pizza, so drop it, okay?" he said sharply.

"Certainly, Mr. Sunshine," she snapped.

"I'm sorry," he said distractedly, "I have a lot on my mind."

"Do you want to talk about it?"

"Later."

The pizza parlor was crowded and noisy, with arcade games being played at full volume. There was little chance for conversation in the din and Jill and Chip only spoke occasionally as they ate. She looked at him often, seeing the frown on his handsome face, and a sense of foreboding had settled over her by the time they returned to the house. The snow was falling heavily, and had changed to thick, wet flakes that were transforming the area into a marshmallow fairyland.

In the house, Chip grumbled about not being able to light a fire in the fireplace in the living room and asked Jill if she wanted a drink. She declined the offer and he joined her in the den with a hefty serving of liquor in his hand. He sat down on the sofa next to her and stared into his glass. Minutes passed, and finally he let out a deep sigh and turned to her.

"Jill," he said, his voice low, "last night when you ran downstairs to see the kittens I saw the sketch pad you left on your bed. Why didn't you tell me you could draw like that?"

"There's nothing to tell. It's just a way for me to capture memories on paper. I had a dream once that—but I really don't dwell on it. It's just something I do for my own pleasure. It's rather embarrassing that you saw it, but it's my fault for leaving it there."

"What was your dream?"

"When I was a little girl in school one of the teachers came to the house to talk to my father. She said I had an artistic talent and should have special training to nurture it. Every Saturday for the rest of the school year I went over to her house and she showed me all the different mediums, like watercolors, oils, acrylics, everything. Somehow, though, I just didn't have a flair for those. It was always my sketches that came to life and she told me that was my inner artistic voice telling me where I belonged."

"Didn't she urge you to continue to develop your talent?"

"Oh, yes, but at the end of the summer she got married and moved away. Before she left town she spoke to my father again and recommended several good art schools. Of course, we never had the money for that, so nothing came of it. I always knew that my father felt so bad that I couldn't pursue it. Just before he died he gave me that sketch pad and pencil set. It was his way of saying he was sorry."

"You're a talented artist, Jill."

"No, I never had the chance to learn, to develop my talent. I spent hours in galleries looking at the work, lugged home every book available from the library, and drew for years on everything from grocery bags to butcher paper, but I don't feel I've progressed any further than when that teacher came to the house. Why are we talking about this? And even more, why has it put you in such a lousy mood?"

"Jill, I took your sketch pad to an expert today. He says you're brilliant and he wants to—"

"You did *what*?" she said, jumping to her feet.

"I had to make sure that you were as good as I thought so you wouldn't be hurt. Mr. Kellis said—"

"You took my sketch pad without asking me? You showed the pictures of my father, you, Zinger, and the others to a stranger? That sketch pad, those drawings, those people are mine. Mine! You had no right to do that, Chip!"

"Jill, I didn't want to get your hopes up. Mr. Kellis says you're fantastic. He wants to display your work in his gallery. Don't you understand what this means?"

"I certainly do! It means you took my private property with no regard for my feelings. Those drawings are like a diary, a personal diary of people who have touched my life. Did you see the one of the old woman? She was a bag lady who used to stop and chat with me and Zinger on the steps. A week after I drew that picture they found her dead in an alley. I can remember her when I look at the drawing. They're for me, Chip. No one else. Me!"

"Jill, please. Calm down."

"No! No one can understand what those pictures mean to me. I'm not sticking them on a wall somewhere for people to pass judgment on whether or not I'm a good artist. It doesn't matter if I am or not."

"Yes it does," he said, getting up and gripping her by the shoulders. "This is your chance. It's here, now. People will buy your work, Jill. You can make a whole new life for yourself. You'll never have to be hungry or cold again. Kellis knows his stuff. He wants to represent you in a showing next month with those drawings and a dozen more he'll need by then. Your dream isn't over. It's just begun."

"I can't," she said, tears spilling over onto her cheeks. "Don't you understand? I buried that dream. I won't leave myself wide open to have people criticize me, tell me I tried to enter a world where I don't belong. I'd have nothing left then. Nothing. I won't allow you to do this to me, Chip."

"It wouldn't be like that," he said, shaking her slightly. "Kellis is the best. He knows what he's doing."

"And what do you get out of this?"

"Me? Jill, all I'm trying to do is get you an opportunity to have the things you deserve and to excel in what you're good at. You're not a house painter. You're an artist! You owe it to yourself to go after this."

"No! I owe it to myself to protect what is mine. Those drawings are private, personal. I will not allow them to be ridiculed by rich people who think they're better than anyone else. You can tell your Mr. Kellis to forget it. I won't do it. I won't."

"Jill, listen to me!"

"No," she said, wrenching free of his grasp. "Leave me alone and let my dream rest in peace. It will never come true. Not that dream, or the pretty yellow dresses, or—Just leave me alone!" She sobbed, running from the room and up the stairs.

"Jill! Oh, my God. What have I done to her?"

Almost blinded by her tears, Jill snatched her sketch pad from the dresser drawer and held it tightly to her breasts as she sank to her knees.

Chip didn't understand, she thought. He just didn't. He and R.J. had worked hard to obtain their goal, but they had known it was within their grasp. Chip had no concept of what it was like to have life stay just beyond reach. The hopes, the dreams danced like shadows in a place she wasn't allowed to enter. He wanted her to step over the threshhold, not realizing that would rob her of her last shred of dignity. She would be sent back to where she belonged with nothing left, her fantasies in shreds. And that was all she had. Her fantasies.

"No, Chip," she whispered. "No."

He meant well, she thought, sinking onto the bed, still clutching the pad. He hadn't intended to hurt her. But it showed so clearly how different their worlds were, how far apart. To him dreams were obtainable simply by going after what he wanted. For her they were peaceful refuges to escape to in her mind for snatches of time when reality became too harsh. To lose her fantasies would be to lose herself, for then she would have nowhere to go when life threatened to crush her.

She loved Chip, but she had to leave his house, his world. She had to go back where she belonged. She'd take her sketch pad of memories and her cat and go home.

Downstairs Chip sank onto the sofa and, resting his elbows on his knees, covered his face with his hands. He had blown it, he thought miserably. Handled it all wrong. But what should he have done differently? Jill wasn't running any risks by showing her drawings. Kellis was positive they would be well received and she would be recognized as a talented artist. He had told her that! She had looked so frightened, panicked, as if everything she had was about to be snatched away from her.

"Damn," he said, pushing himself up and beginning to pace the floor. "I don't understand any of this. It's hers for the taking and she won't go after it."

He didn't blame her for being upset that he'd gone behind her back with the drawings. He hadn't liked doing it, but it seemed the safest way. But that wasn't what was tearing her apart. It was something else, an inner fear of something. She had said so many things he didn't understand. Why would she cling to a dream when it could become reality?

He had to talk to her, he thought. He'd hold her in his arms and comfort her, and then they'd go over it all again. He'd make her see what could be hers and assure her he'd be right by her side through the whole thing. He would? He had to be! She was scared to death. He couldn't drop her in Kellis's lap and walk away. After the showing at the gallery she'd be fine and he'd be free to go on his way. Alone. Without her. Good. Great. That's what this was all about, wasn't it? Dammit, he couldn't think straight!

He strode from the den and bounded up the stairs, only to come to a complete halt outside Jill's bedroom door. There was a light visible beneath the door, but no sound came from within. He raised his hand, hesitating for a moment before knocking softly.

"Jill?" he said. "Please, babe, we have to talk."

"Not tonight, Chip. Not now."

"Jill, don't do this. I'm sorry if I upset you, but I'll

explain everything again and you'll see that there's nothing to be frightened of. I'll be with you, Jill, throughout the whole thing."

"No, Chip, you don't understand. Please leave me alone."

"Jill, open the door!" he said, turning the knob and finding it locked. "This is my house." Cripes, he thought, what a stupid thing to say.

Suddenly the door swung open and Jill was standing before him holding her suitcase.

"Yes, Chip," she said quietly, "this is your house, your world, your space, and you have every right to be here. I don't. I'm going home."

"The hell you are!" he roared.

"Get out of my way."

"No, I will not. You're not leaving, do you hear me?"

"What are you going to do? Tie me to a chair?"

"Jill, please. Let's just sit down and discuss this thing quietly."

"No thank you," she said, pushing past him and going down the stairs.

"Dammit, Jill," he said, hurrying after her. "Why are you doing this to me?"

"To you?" She turned to face him in the entryway. "Chip, my leaving won't have any effect on you excpet that your living room won't be transformed into a hospital. I'm sure you can find another painter to finish the job. But my going will have a very big impact on me. I'm taking my cat and myself, my soul . . . my fantasies. Don't you see? That's all I have."

"Stay with me! Please, Jill," he said, his voice choked with emotion.

She shook her head, blinking back tears as she pulled her jacket out of the closet and tugged it on.

"Wait a minute here," Chip said, seeming to snap out of a trance. "How are you planning on getting all the way downtown?"

"On the bus."

"I'm going to wring your neck," he said, throwing up his hands. "You'll have to transfer about eighty-five times. Do you recall that it is snowing?"

"It doesn't matter."

"Okay, go ahead, and when Cataledge's babies freeze to death *you* explain it to her."

"Oh. I didn't think about that."

"There's a helluva lot of things you didn't think about, Miss Tinsley," he said angrily, grabbing his jacket off the hanger. "Like, for example, how selfish you're being. How little regard you've having for my feelings through all this. Maybe I made a mistake, but heaven knows I didn't set out to hurt you. I admit I don't understand what's going on in your head, but you won't even give me a chance to understand. How dare you tell me your leaving won't affect me. You've got a lot of nerve, lady. The hell with it. Go get in the car and I'll drive you home. No, I'll drive Cataledge home and you can come along for the ride."

"Don't strain yourself," Jill yelled.

"Not another word," he growled. "Do not open your mouth."

"Or what? You'll punch me in the chops?"

"Don't tempt me! You've pushed me right over the edge. You've got three seconds to get in that car!"

"Cataledge—"

"I'll get the damn cat. Now move!"

Never in her entire life, Jill thought wildly, had she seen such a furious man as Chip Chandler was at that moment. Sparks seemed to be flying from his dark eyes and a pulse was beating rapidly by his temple. His jaw was clenched so tightly it was a wonder his teeth weren't crumbling. She definitely had better get herself into that car!

She spun around, stuck her nose in the air, and marched out the front door, grimacing when she heard the steady stream of expletives Chip was muttering. His language made the graffiti on the tenement walls seem mild in comparison.

With Cataledge and her brood in their box on the back seat, Chip backed out of the driveway, skidding immediately on the snow-packed street. After regaining control of the vehicle he drove slowly, leaning forward to see better in the heavily falling snow. The drive to Jill's was made in total silence and seemed endless since Chip drove hardly above a crawl.

"At least Zinger had enough sense to stay inside," he said as he parked in front of the tenement.

"You'd better not leave your car unattended," Jill said.

"I'll carry Cataledge upstairs."

"But—"

"I said . . ."

"All right!"

In Jill's apartment, Chip placed the box on the floor and ran his hand over the back of his neck.

"How much do I owe you for painting the ceiling?" he asked tightly.

"Nothing. I ate tons of your food."

"Hell," he said, pulling out his money clip and tossing several bills on the sofa.

She swallowed the sob in her throat as he stalked to the door and pulled it open.

"I would have tried to understand," he said quietly, looking down at the floor, "if you had given me a chance. You talk about worlds. You're so tightly wrapped up in yours, you won't let anyone in. I'd think it would get awfully lonely in there. Good-bye, Jill. I hope you get your pretty yellow dress someday. I sure as hell would have liked to have been the man who danced with you when you wore your yellow chiffon."

And then he was gone. Without looking at her he left the apartment, shutting the door quietly behind him. She stared at the door, not blinking, hardly breathing, until at last she covered her face with her hands and wept.

When Chip emerged from the building he discovered that all four of his hubcaps were missing. Even more depressing was that he didn't particularly give a damn.

By noon the next day, Jill had made a half-dozen trips up and down the stairs in search of Zinger. She was just returning to her apartment after the seventh try when she met another one of the tenants, Mrs. Rosengren.

"Have you seen Zinger, Mrs. Rosengren?" she asked.

"Haven't you heard, deary? They carted that convict away late yesterday."

"What? Zinger hasn't done anything wrong."

"Not the police, the ambulance people. He fell over unconscious on the front steps."

"Where did they take him?" Jill whispered.

"Charity ward at the county hospital, I suppose." Mrs. Rosengren shrugged. "The man obviously doesn't have a cent to his name."

Jill ran into her apartment and grabbed her coat and the keys to her old panel truck. Outside she moaned in frustration when she turned the key in the ignition and nothing happened.

"Damn," she said. "The battery must be dead." She pushed open the door and ran at full speed to the bus stop on the corner.

An hour later, she was wringing her hands and pacing the floor in the waiting room at the county hospital. The nurse on duty had informed her that, yes, a Mr. Francis Zumwald had been admitted the previous evening. If Jill cared to sit down, the nurse would try to locate someone who could inform her of the patient's condition.

"Hello," a deep voice said from behind her. Jill spun around. "I'm Doctor Lockwood. I understand you're inquiring about Mr. Zumwald."

"Yes. Yes, I am. How is Zinger?"

"Zinger?"

"That's the name he uses. Please, Doctor, I'm so worried."

"Hey, take it easy. Come sit down. Mind if I smoke? I tell all my patients to quit this nasty habit."

"Go right ahead. Aren't you awfully young to be a doctor?"

"I'm thirty-three, but I'm a late bloomer. It's the red hair. I'm still in my cute stage, but I'll be handsome in another year or so. Are you related to Mr.—to Zinger?"

"No, I'm his best friend. His only friend."

"Lucky man."

"How is he, Doctor?"

"Call me Eddie. Who are you?"

"Jill Tinsley."

"Well, Jill Tinsley," Eddie said, taking a deep drag on the cigarette, "your Zinger is a sick man. He had a heart attack, a bad one."

"Oh, God," Jill whispered.

"I've ordered a series of tests because I honestly believe he's going to need surgery. We have some surgeons who volunteer their services, but frankly this hospital isn't equipped to handle heart surgery. He really should be treated by a top surgeon at another hospital, but that's going to take a bit of money, or at least proof of ability to pay."

"When will you have the test results?"

"Should be back in a couple of hours."

"I'll wait."

"Let's go have lunch. The food here is junk, but it's better than nothing."

"No, I don't think—"

"Come on, Jill. Don't argue with a doctor. We're extremely brilliant, which makes us temperamental."

Jill managed to eat half of the meal that Eddie Lockwood placed in front of her and actually found herself relaxing in the friendly man's company. Eddie was good-looking in a wholesome sort of way and had a trim physique on his five-foot-nine- or ten-inch frame. Part of her mind listened to his nonstop chatter, but another part danced between images of Zinger and Chip.

Her dreams the previous night had been haunted by Chip and she had awakened a few times to find tears on her cheeks. She missed him with a painful intensity, ached to see him, to be held in his strong arms. She had been wrong to fall in love with him. The memories of his kiss and touch and throaty chuckle were not going to be enough.

"Hello?" Eddie said, jiggling her arm.

"I'm sorry. I guess I'm not very good company."

"You're the prettiest thing I've seen around here in a long time, Jill Tinsley. You don't have to talk, I'll just stare at you."

"I appreciate what you're doing," she said, smiling slightly. "You're very kind. And thank you for the lunch."

"Such as it was. Tell you what. I've got to get back to work, but I'll come find you in the waiting area the minute I have any news about Zinger."

"May I see him?"

"Not now, honey. I'll sneak you in later, okay?"

"Thank you, Eddie."

"You betcha."

"Eddie?"

"Yeah?"

"Please don't let Zinger die. He's—he's all I have left now," she said, her voice hushed.

"Hang in there, sweetheart. I'll see you later."

She clutched her hands tightly together in her lap and willed herself not to cry, even as two tears slid down her cheeks. She had never in her life felt so incredibly, incredibly alone.

Chip stood at his office window, his forehead pressed against the cold glass as he stared at the bustling city below. After returning to his house the previous night he had drunk himself into oblivion, and he had a killer of a headache to show for it.

"Chip?" R.J. said, coming up behind him.

"Yeah?" Chip said, not moving.

"I just got in from an all-morning biggies' meeting over at—You look lousy."

"Yeah."

"What's wrong?"

"I'm hung over."

"You got drunk?"

"That's putting it mildly."

"Why?"

"Because Jill is gone."

"Gone! What in the hell did you do to her? Dammit, Chip, are you crazy? I knew it! I should never have let you take over. I had this programmed to the last detail, and like an idiot I—"

"What are you talking about?" Chip said, turning to face R.J.

"You and Jill. She's the best thing that ever happened to you, and falling in love with her was the smartest move of your dumb life. I was supposed to be your best man at the wedding."

"You conned me? You set me up?"

"Damn right, and you screwed it up."

"You mean the bit with the flowers and the hearth-and-home number was a scam?"

"Yeah, and you loved every minute of it, right?"

"Right," Chip said, leaning his forehead back

against the window, "and I love Jill, and I don't want to fall out of love with her anymore, but it's too late because she's gone."

"What happened, Chip?" R.J. asked quietly.

"I don't know. I thought I was doing the right thing, but it blew her mind. She's protecting herself, R.J."

"From you?"

"Me, people like me, who would take away her fantasies. That's all she has, you know."

"I don't understand, Chipper."

"I'm not sure I do, either, but maybe I do. She only lives blocks from here, but it's an entirely different world with a separate set of rules. Jill has nothing tangible to hold on to so she allows herself a few fantasies to make the going easier."

"That sounds reasonable."

"R.J., I discovered that Jill is a talented artist. I brought her drawings to Mr. Kellis and he was going to give a showing of her work at his gallery. When I told Jill she fell apart. Her drawings are very private and personal and I infringed on that. I was asking her to live out one of her dreams and it scared her to death. Why? Because if it exploded in her face, she'd have lost it altogether. The fantasy would have become reality, and to Jill reality is a living hell."

"Man," R.J. said, "this is heavy. Where did Jill go?"

"Home, to that hole in the wall."

"Does she know you love her?"

"No. She doesn't even trust me, R.J. I tried to take something very special away from her."

"What are you going to do?"

"I have no idea."

"I'm hating this, Chip."

"And I'll love Jill Tinsley for the rest of my no-good life. You know, I should bust your jaw for conning me."

"Go ahead, if it will make you feel better."

"Forget it. It wouldn't help."

"Couldn't you go talk to her?"

"No, I ruined it. She'll never let me near her again. If it wasn't for knowing that Zinger is there to watch over her, I'd go straight out of my mind."

It was nearly six o'clock before Eddie Lockwood reappeared. Jill got to her feet as the young doctor approached her.

"I'm sorry, Jill," he said. "Everything took longer than I thought."

"What did you find out?"

"Zinger absolutely has to have surgery to correct the damage to his heart. We've got him stabilized for now and I want to build him up some before they operate. He obviously hasn't been eating properly. Like I said, they'll perform the surgery here, but if there was any way you could afford to have him moved to a hospital that specializes in heart surgery . . ."

"Zinger doesn't have any money, and neither do—Wait!" she said suddenly. "I might have something I can sell. Could I let you know tomorrow?"

"Sure."

"May I see Zinger now?"

"No can do. The big brass is milling around and I don't dare sneak you in there."

"All right." She sighed. "But if he wakes up, please tell him I was here and he's not to worry about anything."

"I will."

"Thank you, Eddie. I'll see you tomorrow. Good night."

"Good night, Jill. You sure brightened up my day. Take it easy going home."

Jill got off the bus two blocks from her building and stopped at a small grocery store. She still had not received the check for placing the advertisements on the car windshields, and had no choice but to spend some of the money Chip had tossed onto her sofa. She had to eat and so did Cataledge.

She would have to do it, she thought frantically as she walked home. She would have to try and sell her drawings. There just wasn't any choice now. The sketches would be placed before the public and judgment would be passed. Judgment on the faces of Chip, Zinger, her father? Oh, how she had dreamed of becoming a famous artist, dressing in beautiful clothes and receiving praise from the many people who would flock to see her work. She was crazy to think anyone would want to buy things drawn by a hand no more skilled than when she was a child. But if there was any chance at all that Chip's friend was right, she'd have to take the risk of being ridiculed, stripped bare of her pride, her fantasy. She had to, for Zinger.

A sudden movement in the darkness caught her eye and she saw two tall figures fall into step behind her. Green eyes flashing with anger, she spun around.

"Slicer! Ricky!" she yelled. "I know that's you! It's me. Jill."

"Damn, Jill, we didn't know."

"You were going to snatch my groceries, you yo-yos," she shrieked, stamping her foot.

"Not from you, Jilly," Ricky said. "Hey, don't tell Zinger we scared you, okay? He'll break our kneecaps."

"Oh, guys." She sighed and turned, starting back down the sidewalk. "Zinger is in the hospital."

"No foolin'?" Slicer said as the youths walked on either side of her. "What happened?"

"He had a heart attack and has to have an operation. Want an orange?"

"Yeah," Slicer said, taking two out of the bag and tossing one to Ricky.

"Put the peelings in your pocket," Jill said absently. "This neighborhood is messy enough."

"Jill," Slicer said, biting into the fruit right through the thick skin, "Zinger don't have no money. I bet they just let him croak."

"No!" Jill said. "I'm going to get the money he needs. Somehow."

"Listen, Jilly," Ricky said, "I lifted four wire-rim hubcaps last night off a nice set of wheels in front of your building. I'll fence 'em and get you the cash for Zinger, okay?"

"A car in front of—A late model sedan, sort of bronze colored?"

"Yeah."

"Oh, no," she moaned. "Ricky, that was Chip's car."

"Who?"

"He's a . . . friend of mine. I want those hubcaps back right this minute!"

"Ah, come on, Jilly. I can get big bucks for those."

"*Now*, Ricky!"

"Hell," the boy said, taking off at a run down the street.

"Did you see Zinger?" Slicer asked.

"I was at the hospital but I couldn't visit him. A doctor is going to sneak me in tomorrow. Oh, Slicer, I'm so worried about Zinger. I've got to get some money so he can be moved to a better hospital. I'm going to do it. I swear I will."

"I hope so, Jill. How come you're walkin'? You shouldn't be out here after dark."

"I think the battery's dead in my truck."

"I'll get you a new one."

"Don't steal a battery for me, Slicer."

"I'll borrow one," he said, laughing. "Listen, me and Ricky will look after you while Zinger is away.

Who's this Chip guy? Want us to watch his car when he comes to see you?"

"He won't be over anymore," she said quietly.

"Well, if he shows, we'll make sure no scums mess with his wheels."

"I'm back," Ricky said breathlessly. "I sure could get some bucks for these, Jilly."

"Ricky!"

"Yeah, okay. I'll carry 'em to your room for you."

"We're taking care of Jill for Zinger," Slicer said.

"Yeah, man, no sweat," Ricky said. "Don't worry about nothin', Jilly. Me and Slicer will be around."

"Thank you," she said. "Want to come up and see my cat's new kittens? Zinger is going to take one. He has to be all right. He's got to come home to get his kitten."

"He will," Slicer said, putting his arm around Jill's shoulders. "He will."

"I hope so," she whispered.

The next morning, Jill dressed in her best jeans, the fluffy pink sweater, and braided her hair into a single plait down her back. She emerged from the building to find Slicer sitting on the front steps.

"Hi," the husky youth said. "Where you off to?"

"I have to go see Chip and return his hubcaps and discuss some business. His office is over by the Ren Center."

"I'll walk you over. Some slime might steal those wire rims from you."

He escorted her to the front of Chip's building and handed her the shopping bag containing the hubcaps.

"What's in that tissue package?" Slicer asked. "Is that what you're selling to get money for Zinger?"

"That's the plan. Thanks for bringing me over. I'll see you later."

"Yeah."

When Jill entered the offices of Vestco, Helen looked up. She was surprised to see a pretty young woman with enormous green eyes, wearing a faded pea jacket and carrying a shopping bag.

"May I help you?" Helen asked.

"It's very important that I speak with Mr. Chandler," Jill said. "I don't have an appontment, but I'll gladly wait as long as necessary."

"And your name?"

"Jill Tinsley."

"I'll tell him you're here," Helen said, getting up from her desk.

Jill took a deep breath and gave herself several firm directives. She would not cry when she saw Chip. She would blank her mind of the memories of his kiss and touch. She would not dwell on the fact that she loved him with every fiber of her being. This meeting was strictly business.

"Chip," Helen said, walking into his office, "I know you and R.J. are busy in here, but there's a Jill Tinsley to see you."

"Who?" Chip and R.J. said in unison, both jumping to their feet.

"My goodness," Helen said.

"Jill is here?" Chip said. "Here?"

"Yes, right outside. Who is she?"

"Remember the yellow roses?" R.J. said.

"Oh, I see." Helen nodded. "Well, do I show her in?"

"No! Yes! Oh, man," Chip said, raking his hand through his hair.

"Easy, buddy," R.J. said. "Don't fall apart. Come on, Helen. This will definitely be a private meeting."

R.J. and Helen left the room as Chip straightened his tie and pulled on his jacket. Jill, he thought wildly. Jill was here! Why? Well, he'd keep his mouth shut for a change and wait to see what was going on.

"Hi, Jill," R.J. said. "Nice to see you again."

"Hello, R.J."

"Go on in. Chip is waiting for you."

"Thank you." She walked into Chip's office and closed the door.

"She looks so frightened," Helen said.

"If he blows it this time, I'll kill him," R.J. said, stalking into his office.

"Hello, Chip," Jill said quietly. "I appreciate your seeing me without an appointment."

"Oh, Jill," he said, coming around his desk, "you don't need an appointment to see me. I—"

"I brought your hubcaps back. I'm very sorry they were stolen but . . . the person didn't realize you are . . . a friend of mine. Anyway, here they are."

"Thank you. That's really very nice of you. Jill, I—"

"May I sit down?"

"Yes, of course. You're not dizzy or anything, are you?"

"No." She sat down on the chair opposite Chip's desk and frowned slightly when he drew another up close to hers and sat down.

"Jill, we have to talk."

"This is a business call, Chip. I've—I've decided to turn my sketches over to that man you know. I would have gone there myself but I honestly couldn't remember his name. So, if you'll just tell me where his gallery is, I'll—"

"Why?" Chip asked seriously. "Why are you doing this?"

"Why not?" she said, waving her hand breezily in the air. "Might as well get myself a few bucks so I can live it up."

"You're a lousy liar, Jill. What's going on?"

"Of course, I don't come cheap. I'm going to insist on a cash advance before I give him my work. He'll do that, won't he? Give me some money right now? Of course he will. After all, it's not every day of the week that a gallery owner gets the privilege of displaying the art work of Jill Tinsley. He'll just have to cough up the coins and—"

"Dammit, Jill," Chip roared. "Quit playing games. What kind of trouble are you in?"

Six

That did it.

Jill covered her face with her hands and burst into tears.

"Oh, Lord," Chip moaned. "I've done it again. Jill? Babe? Hey, come on, talk to me. What's wrong?"

"It's Zinger," she said between sobs. "He's sick, very sick. He has to have an operation on his heart. But the doctor said he should go to a better hospital, and they'll need a deposit, or proof of ability to pay, or something."

"How much do you need?" Chip asked, gently pulling her hands away and turning her face toward him.

"I don't even know. I should have asked, I guess. Chip, will that gallery advance me anything at all?"

"I doubt it. It's all figured at time of sale. You get yours and they take a commission. I'll give you the money."

"No! I refuse to take—"

"Hold it, hold it. I'll *lend* you the money until after the showing of your work. How's that?"

"Why?"

"Because I . . . um . . . I like Zinger. He's a good man."

"Well, I suppose that would be all right as long as I sign a promissory note saying how much I owe you."

"For Pete's sake, Jill."

"I insist."

"Okay, whatever you say. Why don't you take off your coat and relax while I make some calls. Can you go see Mr. Kellis at the gallery today?"

"I guess so."

"Would you like some coffee?"

"No, thank you."

"May I kiss you?"

"Yes, please."

And he did. He stood and pulled her into his arms, kissing her with a vehemence that took her breath away. Fresh tears spilled onto her cheeks as she leaned against him, relishing his strength, drinking in his special male aroma.

"Jill," he said, cupping her face in his hands, "I can't lose you again. Not again. I love you, Jill Tinsley. I love you so much I can't find the words to express its depth."

"What?" she whispered.

"I do love you, Jill. I hurt you and I'm so sorry. Please forgive me. Let me into your world, babe. Don't leave me out here all alone. Give me a chance to try and teach you to love me too. I know you don't now, but maybe someday. . ."

"Oh, but I do! I do! I love you, Chip. *You* are my world. I love you!"

"Don't move," he said. "Don't move an inch."

"What?"

"I'll be right back." He ran from the room, past an

astonished Helen, and into R.J.'s office. "She loves me!" he yelled. "Jill loves me!"

"Hot damn!" R.J. whooped, punching his fist in the air. "We did it!"

"Bye," Chip said, sprinting away. "Jill loves me, Helen," he said as he flew past.

"I'm going to cry," Helen said, searching frantically for a tissue.

Chip slammed the office door shut and returned to a wide-eyed Jill, who was very thoroughly kissed before she had a chance to ask him if he'd lost his mind.

"Oh, man," he said, hugging her so tightly she yelped for mercy. "I am the luckiest guy in the world. I swear it, Jill. I swear I'll never again make you cry. Now listen to me, okay? I understand how you feel about those drawings. You don't have to give them to Kellis. We'll figure out another way to get the money for Zinger."

"No, it's all right, Chip. It really is. I don't need my fantasies anymore because I have you. I'll submit my work to Mr. Kellis."

" 'I shall stand alone,' " Chip said softly, " 'and await the one who will meet the needs of my heart and body, and will return such gifts in kind.' "

"You remembered that I said that?"

"Oh, yes, my Jill, I remembered. I'll do that, babe, I'll return your love in kind. I'll cherish every minute we're together."

"Oh, Chip."

They simply stood there. Holding each other tightly, they replaced hurt and confusion with loving thoughts and gentle memories. Seconds stretched into minutes, then Chip reluctantly moved away.

"I've got to get on the phone," he said.

"Yes."

Jill paced the floor nervously while Chip spoke to the nurse on duty at the hospital and was told that

Mr. Zumwald had spent a comfortable night. He then started calling doctors he knew and friends, asking for recommendations for the best heart surgeon in the city. While he spoke to another hospital about available beds, when the surgeon could operate, how they could arrange the payments, Jill walked to the window and stared out at the gray winter day. How was this possible? she wondered, still dazed. Chip loved her! He was honest-to-goodness in love with her. That didn't change the glaring differences in their worlds, but she wouldn't worry about that now. She wanted only to glow in the knowledge that she loved and was loved in return by the most wonderful man on earth. It was almost frightening to be this happy, so euphoric. Nothing must happen to the love she and Chip shared. Nothing.

"All set," he said. "We'll go to the county hospital to see Zinger, grab some lunch someplace, and head out to Kellis's gallery."

"Okay," Jill said, picking up her sketch pad and coat. "Do you want to put your hubcaps on?"

"Later. I'm not even going to ask how you got them back. I'll probably get an ulcer. You've spent your last night in that neighborhood, Jill."

"But I can't leave now. Zinger is going to need care when he comes home from the hospital."

"Let's just take one thing at a time here," he said, circling her shoulders with his arm as they left the office.

"But—"

"Helen," Chip said, "this is Jill. My lady. My love."

"I'm so happy for you both," Helen said, sniffling.

"Hear, hear," R.J. said, coming out of his office. "When is the big day? I'm going to be best man, aren't I?"

"You bet," Chip said.

"Big day?" Jill said.

"Our wedding, my sweet. It will be soon, R.J. Very soon."

"It will?" Jill said, her eyes wide. "We never discussed—"

"We're in a rush, folks," Chip said. "Places to go, people to see. Catch you later."

"Bye," R.J. and Helen chorused.

"Chip," Jill said, when they were driving to the hospital, "you didn't say anything about marriage. I mean, isn't this rather sudden?"

"Jill, I love you. I have never loved anyone before and this is for the rest of my life. I want to marry you, have a family. I guess I should have officially proposed, but I assumed you knew that when I said how I felt about you."

"My mind is whirling. So much is happening so quickly. I'm so concerned about Zinger, and there's this thing with my drawings. Couldn't we talk about getting married when things calm down a little? Just knowing you love me is enough."

"I want you to be my wife, but I realize you have a lot going on right now. We'll wait a bit. Not long though."

"This may sound strange, Chip, but even though we're in love we don't know each other very well. We have so many discoveries to make. Does that make sense?"

"Nope." He smiled. "I love you. I will always love you. The end. You'll probably still be surprising me on our fiftieth wedding anniversary. Don't worry about a thing. You and I together are an unbeatable team."

She laughed. "And Cataledge."

"Oh, yeah, the mama. I'm going to speak to her about her wanton ways. Her days of having children out of wedlock are over."

"She's a good mother."

"And you will be too. I want us to have a daughter that looks just like you."

"Now you're all the way to babies? Chip, slow down here."

"No way. I'm thirty years old and I've waited a lifetime for you. There's no stopping me now. Hey, I'll even go to PTA meetings. How's that?"

Jill just smiled and shook her head, but as she turned to look out the side window a frown creased her brow. She felt as though she were being swept away in a tidal wave. The night before, she had wept tears of loneliness for an unobtainable love, and now? Chip loved her, wanted to marry her, and was talking about babies, for heaven's sake. She couldn't think about all of those things now. Zinger needed her. Just knowing Chip loved her was enough. It warmed her from the tip of her toes to the flush on her cheeks.

At the hospital they went in search of Eddie Lockwood.

"The love of my life," the red-haired doctor said when he saw Jill. "Couldn't stay away from me, huh? Tell me this big dude is your brother."

"Not quite," Chip said, definitely not smiling. "Jill and I are engaged. I'm Chip Chandler."

"You're a lucky man, Chandler. Hell, I was up half the night practicing how I was going to propose to Jill. I missed out again."

"How's Zinger, Eddie?" Jill asked.

"Stable."

"Chip's going to lend Zinger the money for the operation and we've already contacted another hospital that has an excellent heart-surgery team."

"Fantastic. Nice going, Jill."

"May I see Zinger?"

"Five minutes, and try to look like a nurse."

Eddie escorted Jill to double wooden doors and spoke with the nurse on duty, who scowled but nodded as Jill entered.

"Doctor Lockwood?" Chip said, coming up behind the doctor. "Up front. How is Zinger?"

"Not good. Not good at all," he said, turning to Chip. "I'm glad you'll be around for Jill. I don't think Zinger is going to make it."

"But what about the operation?"

Eddie shrugged. "Sometimes we can only do so much. You must know what Jill can handle. You can decide if she should be told right now that things look bad, or let her hold on to the idea that the surgery will do the trick. She seems so fragile. I wouldn't begin to guess what to say to her. I was mulling it over, but now I'll leave it up to you."

"Wonderful," Chip muttered. "I get to make her cry again."

"Love her," Eddie said, walking away, "and make sure you do a damn good job of it."

Jill sank onto the chair next to Zinger's bed and blinked back her tears. The huge man seemed to have shrunk; he appeared frail and old as he lay sleeping, surrounded by ominous-looking equipment.

"Oh, Zinger," she said, covering his hand with both of hers, "why did this have to happen to you? You're so good, so kind. Please get well. Come home to us, Zinger. The kittens are so cute, and you get first pick."

"Jilly?" Zinger said weakly, opening his eyes.

"Yes, it's me. I'm here."

"You doin' okay with Chandler, Jilly?"

"Oh, yes. He loves me and I love him. I'm very happy. All I need now is for you to get better so you can get out of here. Slicer and Ricky are watching over me while you're away."

"Does Chandler want to marry you, Jilly?"

"Yes. Yes, he does."

"Good. That's good. Now I can rest. I'm tired, Jilly, but now you're not alone no more. Thanks for bein' my friend."

"Zinger . . ."

"Your time is up, miss," the nurse whispered.

"Oh, but . . ."

"Shhh, he's sleeping. Come along, dear."

Jill stood up and kissed Zinger gently on the cheek before walking slowly from the room.

"Okay?" Chip asked her when she joined him.

"I guess so."

"I left my home and office phone numbers at the nurse's station."

"Thank you."

"Come on. I'll buy you some lunch. You're white as a ghost."

Outside in the parking lot, Jill suddenly stopped walking.

"Oh, no! No!" she gasped.

"Jill, what—"

"Zinger was saying good-bye. He made sure I was happy and then he—He's going to die! He's giving up!"

"He wouldn't do—"

"Zinger!" she screamed, turning and running back to the hospital with Chip right behind her.

Eddie Lockwood was coming out of the double doors just as she came barreling down the corridor.

"Eddie?" she said, searching his face for a message. "Eddie?"

"Take it easy, Jill," Chip said, putting his hands on her shoulders.

"Eddie?"

"I'm sorry, Jill. Zinger is gone. He just closed his eyes and slipped away."

"Don't say that to me, Eddie," she whispered. "Say anything else, but don't tell me that Zinger is dead."

"Chandler," Eddie said gruffly, "I think you have to help me here."

"Jill," Chip said, turning her to face him, "Zinger was very ill. He probably wouldn't have survived the surgery. He would have hated being cooped up in here much longer, babe. Remember how contented he was to sit outside on the steps? Think about it. He couldn't have liked being here. He's free again, just the way he wanted to be."

"Yes, you're right," Jill said as tears ran down her cheeks. "I'm so glad I drew his picture. I'll always have that, won't I?"

"Yeah, babe," Chip said, "you will. Let's go home. Doctor, I'll make all the funeral arrangements and call back in, okay?"

"That's fine. Good-bye, Jill."

"Thank you for everything, Eddie," she said quietly.

In the car, Jill took a shuddering breath and nestled close to Chip. He kissed her on the top of her head and handed her his handkerchief.

"Do you think you could eat something?" he asked gently.

"Not now. Please take me home. I promised Ricky and Slicer I'd tell them when there was any news."

"Okay," Chip said, turning the key in the ignition. "Slicer? Never mind. I don't want to know. I'm going to stop at a phone booth and cancel the appointment with Kellis. You've had enough for one day."

She nodded and then closed her eyes, trying to halt the flow of tears. Good-bye, Zinger, she thought. Good-bye, dear friend.

Dirty clumps of slush lined the edges of the sidewalks and the sky was gray and heavy with clouds that looked ready to dump a fresh layer of snow on the city at any moment. Jill and Chip rode in silence to the tenement, Jill blanking her mind of thought. She was suddenly tired and drained, and wanted nothing more than to sleep for hours.

"Hoo-boy," Chip said as they neared her building, "we've got company and they don't look too friendly."

Jill straightened and glanced out the window.

"That's Slicer and Ricky. Go ahead and park the car."

"I hope you know what we're doing. Don't get out until I come around for you."

Chip gave the two teenagers what he hoped was a "Don't mess with me, I'm tough" glare and helped Jill from the car.

"Hello, Slicer, Ricky," she said. "This is Chip."

"You got them wire rims ripped off again!" Ricky yelled. "I told you I should have fenced—"

"Ricky," Jill said, "Chip hasn't put them back on yet."

"Are you the one who—" Chip started, only to close his mouth when Jill placed her hand on his arm.

"Jill," Slicer said, "how's Zinger?"

"He—he was too sick," she said quietly. "He died."

"Dammit!" Slicer yelled. "They didn't help him, right? He was busted broke so they just let him croak and nobody gave a damn, right? I'm going down to that place and—"

"No, Slicer," Jill said. "Chip lent me the money for Zinger, but it wouldn't have made any difference. Zinger was so tired and he wanted to go where no one could coop him up again. I talked to him and he wasn't sad or anything. It was crowded in there, Slicer. Zinger wanted to be free."

"You sure them doctors treated him okay, Jilly?" Ricky asked, his voice oddly husky.

"Yes, Ricky. They were nice. They did everything they could. Honest."

Chip swallowed the lump in his throat as he watched Jill hug each of the boys in turn. They seemed to cling to her as they blinked back their tears, and she smiled as she placed a hand on their cheeks. Both Ricky and Slicer cleared their throats noisily and straightened their stances, shoving their hands into the pockets of their jackets.

"We'll watch your car, Chip," Slicer said. "You takin' care of Jill now?"

"No way," Ricky said. "We're in charge of Jilly."

"Jill is my lady," Chip said. "Zinger knew that. He knew I'd never let anything happen to her."

The boys studied Chip for a seemingly endless moment, then Slicer nodded and jerked his head at Ricky, who moved back against the steps.

"We'll watch your car," Slicer said again.

"Thank you," Chip said, wondering absently if a person thanked someone for not stripping their car down to the nuts and bolts. "Let's go upstairs, Jill." Lord, he thought, as they climbed the rickety stairs inside. What a world she'd existed in. Ex-cons and juvenile delinquents, and they adored her, would do battle to protect her from harm. On her word he had been accepted instead of finding himself with a knife at his throat. She had hugged those hoods as though they were grieving little boys, which in a way, he supposed, they were. Jill Tinsley was an incredible woman, and Jill Tinsley was his!

In her apartment she fed Cataledge and picked up each kitten and kissed it on its furry head before finally sinking onto the sofa with a weary sigh.

"Pack some things," Chip said gently, "and I'll take you to my house and you can rest. You're all worn out."

"But . . ."

"We won't discuss anything heavy today, but I need to make some kind of arrangement for Zinger. Do you know what he would have wanted?"

"Not a funeral. We talked about that once. He said he'd like a little thing in the paper saying he was a decent man. That's all."

"I'll take care of it. Come on, babe. Let's go home."

Jill didn't seem to have the energy to think, let alone question Chip's directives, and a short time later they were driving to Westland with Cataledge and the kittens in their box on the back seat. At Chip's she allowed herself to be led upstairs to the frilly bedroom, where he opened her suitcase and handed her the flannel nightgown.

"Get into bed," he said, kissing her on the forehead. "I'll be right downstairs if you need me."

"Thank you so much."

"Shhh. I love you, remember? I'm only doing what's in my job description. Take a nap."

Within moments after slipping on the nightgown and crawling between the sheets, Jill was asleep.

Chip telephoned Helen and dictated a brief paragraph about Zinger which he asked her to submit to the newspaper. After speaking to the person in charge at the hospital, he set a pot of coffee on to drip and leaned against the kitchen counter.

What a day, he thought, pressing the heels of his hands against his eyes. The good with the bad, but the good was here to stay. Jill. He had put Kellis off for a few days with the promise he'd contact him as soon as Jill was over the shock of losing her friend. What would she decide about the drawings now? he wondered. She didn't need the money but, damn, her work should be shown, her talent recognized and appreciated. Well, they'd talk it over later. For now she was there, safe and sound, and she loved him. Everything was going to be fine.

Chip decided against the coffee and set the dial to warm. He walked into the den, tugged off his shoes and jacket, and stretched out on the sofa.

"Fancy meeting you here," he said as Cataledge jumped on his chest and curled up in a ball. "Who's baby-sitting at your place?"

A few minutes later he dozed off with Cataledge moving slowly up and down on his chest to the rhythm of his steady breathing.

When Jill woke she was foggy with sleep and shuffled into the bathroom for a quick shower. Redressed in jeans and a cotton blouse she went downstairs in search of Chip. The light was on in the den, but Cataledge's kittens were the only ones in attendance.

"There you are," she said, finding Chip in the kitchen. "What time is it?"

"Nearly six and we're about to eat. Are you feeling better?"

"Much. What are you cooking?"

"I'll stick these steaks under the broiler now that you're awake, then make a salad, I guess."

"I'll do it."

"Come here first," he said. "I want to kiss you."

Nice, nice, nice, Jill thought, as she raised on tip-toe to receive Chip's searing kiss. It went on and on and her knees dissolved into jelly as she leaned against Chip's rugged body. The last ache of sadness in her heart for Zinger was swept away by the warming emotion of the love she felt for Chip Chandler.

"Salad," he said close to her lips, as he drew a ragged breath.

"Lettuce and stuff," she said dreamily.

"Right."

As they prepared the meal, he told her what he had submitted to the newspaper about Zinger and she stopped tearing the lettuce to place a gentle kiss of gratitude on Chip's cheek. Their eyes met and held in a long, tender gaze that was interrupted by Cataledge sitting on Chip's foot.

"She's hungry," Jill said, snapping out of her trance.

"She's always hungry," Chip said.

"She really likes you, Chip."

"Couldn't she like me from the other side of the room?"

The dinner was delicious and Chip steered the conversation toward lightweight topics and idle chatter. But over one last cup of coffee, Jill suddenly looked worried.

"Was Mr. Kellis upset because we didn't keep the appointment today?" she asked.

"No, he understood. I said I'd contact him in a few days."

"I see," she said, slowly stirring the steaming liquid.

"Things have changed, Jill. You don't need the money you'd get from selling your pictures. You're going to have to get in touch with yourself and decide what you want to do."

"You think I should go ahead with it, don't you?"

"I can't deny that. You have talent and it should be brought before the public. It's really up to you though. If the drawings of your father and Zinger are too personal, you could hold them out for yourself."

"And the one of you. That's mine."

"Kellis looked at that one and told me I was in love with you."

"He did? But *I* didn't know that you were."

"You caught it in my expression somehow but didn't know what you were seeing. That's how talented you are, Jill. You capture the very essence of people on paper. Maybe if you just talked to Mr. Kellis, you'd get a clearer picture of how you feel about all of this."

"Maybe."

"Would you do that? Go out to the gallery with me? I'd be right there with you."

"Well, I guess so. Aren't you spending an awful lot of time away from the office?"

"Don't worry about it."

"Oh, heavens, I've got to finish painting your living room."

"Well, the truth of the matter is, I've changed my mind about the white-white. The ceiling is okay, but I think I'll leave the walls like they are."

"You're kidding."

"No, I threw all the junk back in the garage and canceled the project. It doesn't even smell anymore. We'll clean up here and go make a nice fire in the living room."

"You're keeping the gloom-and-doom room like it was?"

"Yep."

"You're weird."

"Yep."

"I think I've been had."

"I think you're very loved. In fact, I know you are."

"So are you."

The fire in the hearth crackled in a warming glow of leaping orange flames as Jill snuggled next to Chip on the sofa. He untangled her braid and spread the ebony hair across her shoulders and over her breasts.

"Please don't ever cut your hair," he said softly. "Promise?"

"Sure. I'll let it grow down to my toes."

He cupped her face in his hands and turned her toward him, covering her mouth with his in a sweet, sensuous kiss that brought a quiet moan from Jill. The kiss intensified, then he lifted his head abruptly, and moved her away from him.

"I'm sorry," he said. "I just can't handle this tonight. I want you too much, Jill. I'd better not kiss you right now."

The greatest inner peace that Jill had ever known swept over her. She stroked her fingertips down Chip's face and smiled at him tenderly when he turned to look at her.

"I love you, Chip," she said, her voice hushed. "You are my life. I want you to make love to me. Now. Tonight."

"Oh, Jill," he said, pulling her roughly into his arms. "Oh, my Jill."

He stood and checked the screen in front of the fire, then extended his hand to her and led her up the stairs. In his bedroom he turned on the bedside lamp, sending a rosy glow over the large room. The massive, hand-carved bed was covered by a choco-late-brown velvet spread, and a picture of a waterfall hung above it.

"It's lovely," Jill said.

"It's our room now. You can make any changes you like," Chip said. "Are you frightened, Jill?"

"No."

"I'll try not to hurt you, but the first time isn't always the best. Do you trust me, darling? Later it will be beautiful, you'll see."

"Yes, I trust you and I love you."

With a throaty moan, he kissed her, pulling her to him and crushing her breasts against his hard chest. She put her arms around his neck and moved closer, delighting in the feel of his arousal. His body held such promises, such treasures of unknown joys and discoveries, and she wanted it all.

With trembling fingers, he unbuttoned her blouse and brushed it away to fall to the floor, her bra following. His hands cupped her full breasts and he bent his head to draw first one then the other nipple into his mouth. Jill tipped her head back and closed her eyes as desire swirled through her body.

Chip reached for the button on her jeans and swore under his breath when his shaking hands fumbled over the stubborn closure. Jill stepped back and unzipped them herself, pushing them down with her bikini panties and standing before him naked.

"You are so beautiful," he said, his voice raspy. "So beautiful."

She drank in the sight of his body as he hastily removed his clothes. His muscles were taut and glistening with perspiration. Each part of his rugged body complemented the next, and she imagined him as a bronze statue standing majestically in the center of an enchanted city. But he was a man, her man, and the bold announcement of his arousal gave evidence to his masculinity.

"Come to me, Jill," he said, extending his hand to her.

And she went.

He lifted her onto the bed and stretched out next to her, not touching her for a moment as he strove for control. Then, as lightly as a butterfly's wing, he kissed her eyes, cheeks, the slender column of her throat, until moving at last to her breasts that were aching for his tantalizing touch.

She sank her hands into the night darkness of his hair, urging him closer as sweet passion shot through her. One hand still clutching his head, her other roamed over the corded muscles of his back, feeling them tremble under her foray.

His hand slid to the inner warmth of her thigh, stroking and caressing as his mouth continued to devour the lush fullness of her breasts. The flame of desire within Jill raged out of control and she arched her back, seeking more, wanting more. Her breath was coming in short gasps and she felt herself losing touch with reality, time, and space.

"Chip, oh please," she whispered. "I can't . . . I don't understand . . ."

"I'm here, babe," he said, his voice sounding strange to her ears. "Don't be frightened. Go with what you're feeling. Trust me, Jill."

He reached in the drawer of the night stand and quickly prepared himself. He claimed her mouth, his questing tongue delving deep into the inner darkness as he moved over her.

"Hold on to me," he murmured. "It will only hurt for a moment, I promise. Hold on."

A sharp cry escaped her as a searing pain ripped through her, and she gripped Chip's shoulders like a vise. He waited, not moving, until he felt her relax beneath him, and then slowly, slowly, began the ritual as ancient as humankind. Instinctively, Jill moved with him, matching his rhythm perfectly. She was entering a place she had never been and Chip was with her. Higher they climbed, and Jill sensed some unknown goal just out of reach.

And then she was there. Wave after wave of ecstasy rippled through her body. She called to Chip and he answered, shuddering above her as he chanted her name like a litany. He collapsed against her, burying his face in the fragrant cloud of her silky hair. Pushing himself up to rest on his arms, he gazed anxiously at her flushed face.

"Jill? Are you all right?" he asked, concern evident in his voice. "I'm sorry I hurt you."

"It was wonderful!" she said, smiling up at him. "Oh, Chip, it was just wonderful!"

"You gave of yourself totally, Jill. I love you so much."

"I feel so—so . . . Let's do it again."

He chuckled and moved away, pulling her close to his side. "We will," he said. "Just give me a few minutes to recuperate."

"I never imagined in my wildest fantasies that making love would be like this," she said softly. "I feel complete, whole, as if a part of me I never knew has awakened. I'm so glad I waited for you, Chip. So glad."

"You gave me the greatest gift you can give a man. I'll cherish that forever. Thank you, Jill. You are truly mine now. Forever."

They lay quietly together, hands resting possessively on each other. They were lost in their own thoughts, reliving the beauty of what they had just shared. Finally Jill stirred and ran her fingers down Chip's chest, smiling as she felt him tense under the feathery touch.

"Did you recuperate yet?" she asked.

"Oh, yes, ma'am," he said, rolling on top of her. "I certainly did."

"Oh, good!" She laughed. "I'm really getting addicted to this stuff."

"I'm definitely glad to hear that," he said, then boldly took possession of her mouth.

Much, much later they wandered downstairs for mugs of hot chocolate. Chip had pulled on a pair of jeans and Jill was wearing one of his Michigan State T-shirts. It fell to midthigh on her and she said she looked ridiculous. He declared her to be absolutely gorgeous and she decided not to argue the point. They checked the house for the night, bid Cataledge good night, then walked arm in arm back up the stairs.

Jill was yawning as she crawled back into bed after being told to give back the T-shirt. Chip declared he was not sleeping with someone who looked like Dopey the Dwarf. They nestled together, naked but warmed by the heat from their entwined bodies. Chip kissed Jill gently on the forehead and within minutes she drifted off into a peaceful slumber.

Chip lay in the darkness, his precious treasure held safely in his arms. He frowned as he remembered his determination not to love this woman, to rid himself of her and the tempestuous emotions she evoked in him. What a fool he had been, he thought. He'd almost lost her. How would he have survived without her? What purpose would life have held? But now she was where she belonged, and he would give her everything she had been denied in the past. Would she agree to exhibit her drawings? He hoped so. He wanted the world to know how talented Jill Tinsley was. His Jill. His.

"I love you, my sweet," he whispered, then closed his eyes and gave way to sleep.

*　　*　　*

Jill realized she was being kissed and despite her lethargic state decided it was a delicious way to wake up. She opened her eyes and matched smile for smile with Chip Chandler.

"Hello," he said. "How's life?"

"Fantastic," she said, kissing her fingertips.

"Plant one of those right here," he said, pointing to his mouth.

"Oh, you're all dressed up for work. Darn."

"Are you going to kiss me or not?"

"Goodness, you're crabby," she said, sitting up and wrapping her arms around his neck.

"Oh, man," he moaned as the sheet slid down, revealing her bare breasts.

She kissed him with such exuberance he finally had to untangle her arms and push her firmly back against the pillows.

"Don't move," he said, yanking the sheet up to her chin. "I'll be back in seven or eight hours."

She laughed. "Silly man. Come to think of it, what am I going to do all day?"

"Rest, eat, play with the kittens."

"Not enough. You sure you don't want me to paint the living-room walls?"

"Positive. Jill, last night was . . . It was . . ."

"I know. I feel the same way. I love you, Chip."

"And I love you. I'm off to earn my keep. I'll call you later, okay?"

"Yep."

After one more lengthy kiss, Chip said good-bye and walked from the room muttering about the injustices of having to go to work when he could be spending the day in bed with her. She laughed softly and headed for the shower. As she stood under the streaming water, she realized her breasts were tender from the exquisite lovemaking with Chip. She ran her hands over them, remembering the ecstasy his touch had brought.

"Naughty, naughty," she said as a shaft of desire pierced her. "Think about something else. Like, what am I going to do with myself all day?"

As she dressed she realized the situation was far from humorous. She really had nothing to occupy her time and the hours stretched before her like a void. She didn't have to hustle out to try to find an odd job to put money in her pocket, and there was no Zinger to talk to. She was warm and safe, in a beautiful home with plenty of food, and she was absolutely, positively bored out of her mind.

Seven

When Chip telephoned Jill just after lunch, she smiled for the first time since he had left her that morning.

"What's wrong?" he asked. "You sound down."

"I'm so bored, Chip."

"Oh," he said, sounding surprised. "Couldn't you read a book or something?"

"Well, I—"

"Damn, I've got to go. Helen is waving at me because my next client is here. We'll talk about this tonight. Love you, babe. Bye."

"I love—" Jill began, then hearing the dial tone, added, "you too," as she dropped the receiver into place.

Bored? Chip thought, shrugging into his jacket and straightening his tie. She had that great big house to mess around in, and Cataledge and the kittens, and she was bored? What did other women do at home all day? Take care of their babies. Great. He had the perfect solution to the problem. They'd get married right away and—

"Chip?" Helen said from the doorway.

"Show him in, Helen."

Jill flopped onto the sofa and stared at the ceiling. Read a book? she thought. Wonderful. Then what? Watch soap operas? This was nuts. She should be ecstatic having so many carefree hours at her disposal with no worries, but, darn it, she was bored, bored, bored. "Read a book, Jill," she said, pushing herself to her feet, "and count your blessings."

The long afternoon did nothing to improve her mood. The mystery novel she found on a bookshelf held her attention briefly, but she was soon wandering through the large home in search of something to do. She dusted what was already clean, rearranged the living-room furniture, then put it all back the way it had been, deciding she had no right to change Chip's house around. The stiff lectures she delivered to herself on her ungrateful attitude only gave her a headache.

Jill Tinsley was not in a terrific frame of mind.

The aroma of baking pork chops greeted Chip when he came through the front door just after six, and he smiled as he hung up his coat. Man, he thought, how great it had been to turn onto his street and see the lights on in the house in a warm, welcoming glow. And in about two seconds he would pull Jill into his arms and . . . "Jill!" he yelled, heading for the kitchen.

"Hi," she said, hugging him when he entered the room.

The kiss was long and lovely and left them breathless.

"Something smells good," Chip said when he finally released her.

"Me."

"Oh, yeah? You wear pork-chop perfume? It really turns me on."

She laughed. "Go change your clothes. Dinner will be served."

Chip returned to the kitchen a few minutes later clad in jeans and a Michigan State sweat shirt that had seen better days. He helped Jill carry the food to the table, then groaned after they were seated.

"Why is it," he said, "that every time I sit down to eat, Cataledge goes to sleep on my foot?"

"I don't know. I guess you have a comfortable foot. How was your day?"

"Top-notch. R.J. and I sold some condos and turned a profit like you wouldn't believe. Big bucks, my sweet, big bucks. We should be out celebrating. In fact, we'll do just that very soon. R.J. can round up one of his luscious blondes and we'll make it a foursome."

"Luscious blondes?"

"He has a thing for blondes. It's dumb because he and his date always look like the Bobsey Twins."

"Well, you and I both have dark hair."

"Yeah, but we're gorgeous and R.J. is ugly."

"He is not. He's a hunk of stuff."

"Really? I could have sworn he was ugly as sin and the blondes of Detroit simply had no taste. This dinner is delicious. You have just so many talents," he said, wiggling his eyebrows at her.

"Do tell."

"Show and tell is more fun. We will rendezvous in our king-sized bed later, my dear. So! Your day was not earth shattering, huh?"

"I'm not cut out for a life of leisure, Chip. I know I should be grateful . . ."

"Now hold it. Gratitude doesn't have a place in our

relationship. We're based on love, Jill. You've got to remember that I'm older than you are, and I've had more years to work at accumulating material things. We're pooling our resources and sharing fifty-fifty."

"I didn't add anything to the pot."

"Yes, you did. You gave me Jill Tinsley and that's all I need. Cataledge comes under liabilities, but I'll forgive you. Damn, I wish she'd get off my foot. Anyway, back to the subject. You need something to occupy your time."

"Definitely."

"Well, how about a baby?"

"A baby. A baby? We're not even married!"

"A situation that can be remedied in a few days. Blood tests, license, and off we go. Jill, I'm serious. Will you marry me right away so we can really start our life together?"

"Yes."

"Pardon me?"

"Yes, I'll marry you. Why do you look so shocked?"

"I guess I thought you'd want to wait. Man, this is fantastic! We'll call my parents in Florida after dinner. Oh, and my sister. Okay?"

"We're not going to do a fancy number are we? I mean, can't we just go to the courthouse?"

"Whatever you want. Jill, can we talk about the baby?"

"Chip, I love the idea of having your baby, but even if I got pregnant right now—"

"Good idea. Let's go upstairs."

"Stop it." She laughed. "This is important."

"Sorry. Carry on."

"Chip, it takes nine months to have a baby. I'll go crazy by then, and don't tell me to knit booties because all I know how to do is afghans."

"Okay, I understand. Tomorrow is Saturday and we'll go over to your apartment and get the rest of your things. Then we have a two o'clock appointment with Mr. Kellis. If you decide to exhibit your work, you'll be busy doing the other drawings he wants."

"That's true," she said thoughtfully.

"Just keep an open mind when we're talking to him. Am I pushing you about a baby, Jill?"

"No, not at all. To quote a brilliant man, we will rendezvous in our king-sized bed later and get this show on the road."

"You're wonderful," he said, smiling at her tenderly.

"When we go to my place tomorrow I want to say good-bye to Ricky and Slicer."

"Sure. If they're not around, we'll check all the dark alleys. Slicer. What a name. No, don't tell me how he got it."

"It has to do with tires."

"I told you not to tell me!"

After dinner, Chip called his parents and sister with the news of his and Jill's impending marriage. Mrs. Chandler was disappointed that they weren't planning a large, formal affair, but said they'd fly up from Florida to witness the ceremony. Chip's sister proclaimed she would attend with her entire crew in tow. Chip insisted that Jill speak to his family and she did so reluctantly, finding herself shy trying to chat with strangers.

"They're thrilled," Chip said after hanging up the phone. "Why do women always cry when they're happy? My mother came unglued and my sister wasn't much better."

"It's a privilege of our gender."

"Oh. Come sit on the sofa."

"This is nice," she said, snuggling next to him.

"I'm taking you shopping for clothes on Sunday."

"Chip . . ."

"I want you to have nice things."

"I can't afford that much."

"You're about to become my wife! Everything I have

is yours. What are you going to do? Send me a bill for cooking my dinner? I'm going to buy you a beautiful yellow dress."

"I don't think they have yellow dresses in the stores in the dead of winter."

"We'll find one. Would you like to be married in a pretty yellow dress?"

"Oh yes, that sounds lovely."

"Then it's settled. We'll get you all kinds of stuff."

"I don't know about this. Maybe after we're married I'll feel more comfortable about spending your money."

"Our money."

"Oh, Chip." She sighed. "This is all so difficult for me. I've always had to work so hard for everything and I don't know how to accept gifts very graciously, I guess. I felt almost like an intruder here today, as though I shouldn't be touching your things. I wish so much I was more sophisticated, could just walk into your world as if I belonged."

"Dammit, Jill, you *do* belong here. You're with *me* now and that's all that counts. I don't ever again want to hear you putting yourself down."

"I'm not! I'm facing facts."

"You're making me angry. Jill, you are the warmest, most wonderful—Look, would you like me to round up some of the women I've dated so you can see how terrific you are in comparison?"

"Over my dead body, Chandler!"

"I love being over your body, but I prefer it very much alive. Hey, where do you want to go on a honeymoon?"

"Honeymoon?"

"The trip husbands and wives go on after they're married? R.J. can cover for me for a few days. He goes off on honeymoons all the time."

"Huh?"

"Relatively speaking. I think he's practicing until

he gets it right. He's going to wear himself out before he's thirty-five. Anyway, where do you want to go?"

"I have no idea. I've never been out of the thriving metropolis of Detroit."

"Do you want me to surprise you?"

"I love surprises."

"Then leave it to me. How's this for a surprise? Let's go to bed."

"Now?"

"I'm tired, very, very tired."

"Oh, in that case I'll cancel my plans."

"What plans?"

"To make love in front of the fire. To slip my hands under your weird sweat shirt . . . like this. And to lean against your sexy body . . . like this. Then I was going to . . . But if you're tired . . ."

"Lord," Chip groaned, and smothered her bubble of laughter with an urgent, delectable kiss.

Much later they lay nestled together on the carpet, gazing into the dancing flames. Chip drew his sweat shirt over Jill's naked body and kissed her gently on the forehead.

"You were wonderful," he said softly.

"That is a very special place we go to together, Chip."

"Indeed it is, and that is where our child will be conceived. My mother told me once that babies were made in heaven. Now I understand what she meant. Well, actually, it was a phony answer because she thought I was too young to know about sex, but I like the way it sounds."

"So do I," Jill said, trailing her fingertips down his chest.

"Madam, if you don't quit doing that, you are going to be in a heap of trouble."

"I'll live dangerously, Mr. Chandler. Unless, of course, you need to recuperate."

"Nope. I'm more than ready to go to heaven with you again, my sweet. More than ready."

Sometime later, Chip nudged a dozing Jill and led her up the stairs to their room. She fell instantly back to sleep, her head resting on his chest.

Light snow flurries were falling the next morning when Chip parked in front of Jill's building and assisted her out of the car. Ricky and Slicer materialized almost immediately and Jill told them she was moving to Chip's house.

"We'll miss you, Jilly," Ricky said.

"Yeah." Slicer nodded. "Oh, your truck is working."

"Slicer, I told you not to steal a battery for me."

"Oh, Lord," Chip muttered.

"I didn't!" Slicer said. "I checked it over and the cable was loose, that's all."

"Oh, well, thank you," Jill said. "You're welcome to the furniture in my apartment. You could probably get a little money for it if you sold it. And listen, you guys, please take care of yourselves. It'll break my heart if you end up in jail."

"We won't, Jilly," Ricky said. "We can run faster than any cop on this beat."

"That wasn't quite the answer I had hoped for," she said, laughing as she gave them each a hug. "Goodbye."

Upstairs in Jill's apartment, Chip felt a knot tighten in his stomach when he saw that the full extent of Jill's possessions fit into two small cardboard boxes. He convinced her not to bother with her meager house-painting supplies and she agreed reluctantly.

Damn, he thought, he was going to get her everything she had ever wanted. Every dream, every fantasy she had ever had was going to come true, starting with a pretty yellow dress.

"What about my truck?" she asked, after they'd put the boxes in the trunk of his car.

"Let's leave it for now. I want to go buy wedding rings, have lunch, and head out to the art gallery."

"I took the pictures of you, my father, and Zinger out of the sketch pad before we left the house."

"That's fine, babe. You don't have to do anything that doesn't feel right. Ready to go?"

"Yes," she said quietly, turning to look at the empty stairs where Zinger had always sat. "I'm ready."

The wedding rings were brushed gold, Chip's twice as wide as Jill's to look appropriate on his large hand. He had felt her tense up the moment they had entered the exclusive jewelry store and had planted her in front of a display case while he went in search of the manager. There was to be no mention of prices in front of Jill, Chip told the man firmly. None.

During lunch, Jill asked Chip so many times if she could see the rings just one more time, that he finally laughed and set them in plain view in front of her plate.

"Oh, you're getting married," the waitress said.

"Yep," Chip said, looking extremely pleased with himself, "and we're going to have a baby too." Jill rolled her eyes and blushed crimson.

During the drive to the art gallery, Chip glanced over at Jill many times, seeing her grip on the sketch pad tighten with every passing mile. Her green eyes suddenly appeared very large and she was chewing on the inside of her cheek.

"Relax, babe," he said. "I'm right here. You're not alone, Jill. You've got to remember that."

She nodded, but stared straight ahead, her back rigid. She was scared to death, she thought dismally. What was she doing here? Her drawings could not possibly be that good. But Mr. Kellis had said . . . What if he were wrong and the public sneered at the gall of the untrained young artist who had attempted to stake a claim on a world in which she didn't belong? Since she was a child she had dreamed of a moment like this, a chance to step forward and proudly display her talents. That had been her fantasy and now here it was. But dreams were safe havens, reality could be cruel and harsh.

But not always, she argued with herself. She had the love of her wonderful Chip and she was going to have "a pretty yellow dress," she said aloud.

"Dozens of them," Chip said, smiling at her. "A closet full. Is that what you were thinking about?"

"My mind is like scrambled eggs. I'm terribly frightened, Chip."

"I know, babe. I can tell. Do you want to go home?"

"No. I said I'd at least listen to what Mr. Kellis had to say and I will."

"Good for you. There's the gallery up ahead on the right."

"I suddenly have a great deal of sympathy for Marie Antoinette."

Chip chuckled softly and turned into the parking lot as Jill held the sketch pad tightly against her breasts.

Inside the building, Chip led her down a carpeted hallway to the left of the main gallery. Her eyes had widened when they'd entered and she had seen the paintings on the walls, accentuated by specially placed lights. Several pieces of sculpture sat on marble pedestals throughout the room, and the entire effect was airy, uncluttered, and highly professional. Chip introduced them to the secretary and they were shown immediately into Mr. Kellis's office.

"Chip," the owner said, smiling as he got to his feet, "glad you could make it. And you must be Jill Tinsley."

"Yes, I am."

"I'm very pleased to meet you, Jill. Please, both of you, sit down."

"I hope you'll excuse our attire, Mr. Kellis," Chip said, after they were seated, "but we had a busy day of chores and errands."

"No problem," Mr. Kellis said, smiling. "You two look more comfortable in your jeans than I am in this suit."

Jill looked quickly over at Chip as she felt her cheeks grow warm. It had never occurred to her that she was dressed improperly for a meeting like this. She'd pulled on jeans, a blouse and sweater, braided her hair, and sauntered out the door. Why hadn't Chip told her that she should dress up a little? Because he knew the jeans were all she owned, she answered herself. So he hadn't said a word to her and smoothed it over in front of Mr. Kellis. Oh, hell's bells, what was she doing here?

"Mr. Kellis," Chip was saying, "perhaps you could explain to Jill exactly what plans you have in regard to her work."

"Certainly. Jill, I was extremely impressed with your drawings. You have a natural flair and the ability to capture human emotions on people's faces. Right, Chip?"

"Right," Chip said, shifting in his chair.

"I would like," Mr. Kellis continued, "to display your drawings along with the work of two other unknown artists we have discovered. One of them is a metal sculptor, the other works in oils. Your pencil drawings will add the perfect balance. Our gallery will mat and frame your work. Invitations will be sent out to our patrons and other well-known citizens of Detroit for a black-tie opening on the first of March."

"Classy," Chip said, looking over at Jill. She just stared back at him rather blankly.

"Jill," Mr. Kellis said, "I'm sure you can understand that we can't command a tremendous price for your work at this point, since this is a sort of launching pad for you. We'll offer your drawings for two hundred dollars apiece."

Jill gasped. "I beg your pardon?"

"Hopefully," Mr. Kellis said, "we'll be able to ask much more once you've become established."

"Two hundred dollars apiece?" she whispered.

"Of course, our commission is deducted from that."

"Chip? Did he say two hundred or two dollars?"

Chip chuckled. "Two hundred. Does that sound reasonable?"

"It's ridiculous," she said. "Who would pay that kind of money for my work? I don't mean to be rude, Mr. Kellis, but I think you're totally out of your mind."

Mr. Kellis appeared rather startled, then laughed loudly as Chip struggled to suppress a smile.

"I want to go home, Chip," Jill whispered.

"Relax, babe. You're doing fine."

"Oh, ha!" she said, folding her arms over her breasts.

"Jill," Mr. Kellis said, shaking his head, "you are marvelous, absolutely refreshing. And, I think you have no idea how talented you are. So, my dear, do we have a deal?"

"Well, I . . ."

"I told Chip that I would want a dozen drawings in addition to those in your sketch pad. Does that present a problem?"

"I kept three of those out, Mr. Kellis. They were very personal to me."

"That's fine. Then I'll require fifteen additional ones to bring it back up to the number I want. Agreed?"

"I guess so."

"Splendid. Excuse me just a moment and I'll instruct my secretary to draw up the contract," he said, and left the office.

"I can't believe this, Chip," Jill said, shaking her

head. "I'll be laughed right out of Detroit when people see the price on those drawings. This is a terrible mistake."

"No, it's not," he said, reaching for her hand. "Kellis is the best. He knows exactly what he's doing. Would you like me to read the contract before you sign it?"

"Would you?"

"Of course. Do you feel pressured by having to supply fifteen more pictures so soon?"

"I don't know. I've never drawn under any kind of time limit. I'll have to wander around and try to find interesting subjects. I don't even have any supplies, though."

"We'll get them, but we'll thoroughly discuss where you'll be doing your wandering. I don't want you back in your old neighborhood."

"There are some beautiful faces down there."

"No way. We'll talk about this later."

"All set," Mr. Kellis said, coming back into the office. "It's a fairly standard contract, and I've added the number of drawings we'll need and that they're to be delivered in groups of three or four so we can keep up with the framing. The last are to be here no later than two days before the exhibit."

"May I?" Chip said, extending his hand for the contract. He read through it all, asking Mr. Kellis to clarify a few points. "Looks fine," he finally said.

"Jill?" Mr. Kellis said, placing a pen on the edge of the desk.

Jill reached tentatively for the pen, very aware that her hand was trembling. Sign it, Jill, she told herself firmly. Sign the damn contract! She knew how much Chip wanted her to do this, but what about herself? Did she really wish to place herself at the mercy of a possibly harsh and critical public? No! But how was she to fill the idle hours of her new life? She desperately needed something to challenge her, give her a sense of accomplishment.

"Jill?" Chip said softly. "It's up to you. Yes or no?"

Taking a deep breath, Jill scribbled her name on the contract, then dropped the pen as if it had singed her fingers.

"Thank you," Mr. Kellis said. "May I have the sketch pad, Jill?"

"Now?" she asked. "Yes, of course you want it now. Here you are, Mr. Kellis, and I'm very grateful for everything you're doing for me."

He laughed. "Even though you think I'm crazy? Don't you worry about a thing. Our gallery goes all out for its artists. Oh, here is the name and address of the photographer who'll be taking your picture for the catalogue. You have an appointment at ten Monday morning. I hope that's convenient."

"Photographer?"

"She'll be there," Chip said, getting to his feet and extending his hand to Mr. Kellis. "Thank you, sir."

"Give my best to your parents," the older man said. "See you soon, Jill."

"Yes. Good-bye," she said as Chip gripped her elbow and led her to the door.

In the car, Jill pressed her hands to her burning cheeks. "What have I done?" she said.

"You've made a very positive step toward an exciting career, my sweet," Chip said, turning the key in the ignition. "That wasn't so bad, was it?"

"It was grim. Why didn't you tell me I was dressed all wrong?"

"It doesn't matter. Mr. Kellis is a good ol' boy. He doesn't care about stuff like that. We're getting you new clothes tomorrow, which will include something really special for the exhibit. Oh, yeah, and an outfit for your photography session."

"This is just too much," she said. "Why do I have to have my picture taken?"

"That's show biz, kid."

"Ugh."

Although Chip was far from pleased with the plan, they drove back down to the tenement so Jill could follow him home in her truck. He raised his brows when he saw the ancient vehicle, but remained silent. The trip to Westland took three times as long as usual as Chip seemed convinced the truck would fall apart if driven over twenty miles an hour.

At the house, they carried the boxes of Jill's belongings upstairs and Jill hesitated in the corridor.

"*Our* room is at the end of the hall," Chip said.

"I could still leave my clothes in the guest room so I wouldn't crowd you."

"Nope. March."

"Brother," Jill said, sticking her nose in the air as she walked down the hall.

"Art supplies," Chip said the next morning after breakfast as he flipped through the Yellow Pages. "Who in the heck carries art supplies around here?"

"When Mr. Kellis said it was black tie, does that mean you'll wear your penguin suit?" Jill asked as she wiped off the kitchen counters.

"Yep."

"So, I'd have to have a very fancy dress?"

"Yep."

"Black satin?"

"Nope."

"Why not?"

"Because I distinctly remember telling you that was what my date was wearing the night I came to your apartment. Don't try to be something you're not, Jill. Just be yourself."

"Myself wears jeans."

"We'll find just the right thing for you. Here we go. Art supplies."

"Oh, Chip," she said, sitting down opposite him, "all this is going to cost so much money."

"Don't start that again," he said. "It's getting old. Whatever I have is yours, and the subject is closed. Now, go feed Cataledge and then we'll hit the road."

She opened her mouth to protest, but when she saw the hard set to Chip's jaw, she decided to feed the cat. Maybe, just maybe, she told herself, she'd feel more a part of all this when she had some money of her own from the sale of the drawings. *When* she sold the drawings? Not hardly. It was definitely a very big "if."

Chip was thoroughly enthralled by the supplies in the art store and asked Jill a steady stream of questions, such as why she selected a particular type of paper and pencils. No, she said, she didn't want an easel or fancy smocks, thank you, and had to tell Chip three times that she was ready to leave.

"Neat stuff," he said, looking back over his shoulder as they left the store.

The next stop was a well-known women's boutique and Chip breezed in as if he did such things every day of his life.

"Hello," he said to the saleswoman, flashing her a dazzling smile. "My wife needs some new clothes. Everything from the inside out."

"Chip, for heaven's sake," Jill said.

"And," he added, "we must have a yellow chiffon dress."

"I'm sorry, sir," the woman said. "Our yellows will be coming in with the spring line. We show darker shades in winter."

"Doesn't anyone have yellow chiffon now?"

"I doubt it."

"Well, damn. Okay, let's see what you have. I'll sit in one of those little chairs over there and we'll all play fashion show."

"Splendid," the saleswoman said.

"Ridiculous," Jill muttered.

"Somewhere in Detroit, Michigan, there is a yellow chiffon dress," Chip whispered in Jill's ear.

"Shhh," she said.

For the next half hour Jill was put into and taken out of various creations, all of which Chip rejected with a decisive shake of his head.

"Oh, man, that's nice," he said finally, when she emerged from the back room in a street-length dress of soft cranberry-colored wool. "That's perfect for the photography session. Do you like it?"

"It's lovely."

"Good. Next!"

"Is he always like that?" the saleswoman asked Jill.

"Most of the time," she said, laughing. "Now I have to have something fancy, but it can't be black satin."

"Orders from headquarters?"

"Absolutely."

When Jill appeared in a teal-blue floor-length dress that scooped to just above her breasts and hugged her slender hips, Chip got to his feet and stared at her. He simply stared.

"You are the most beautiful woman I have ever seen," he murmured.

"But, Chip, it costs—"

"We'll take it," he said. "Oh, and some shoes to go with these. Are you sure you don't have yellow chiffon?"

"Well, I suppose I could call around for you," the saleswoman said.

"Great. It has to have long sheer sleeves."

"You remembered how I described my fantasy dress!" Jill said, placing her hand on his arm.

"Yes, babe, I remembered."

That night after Chip was asleep, Jill pulled on the Michigan State T-shirt and went down the hall to the guest room where the yellow chiffon dress was hanging in a plastic bag in the closet. She carefully lifted it free and held it in front of her, smiling at her reflection in the mirror.

It was so beautiful, she thought. Even more lovely than the one she had dreamed about. And it was her wedding dress, which made it even more special. That poor saleswoman had made twenty calls before finding the dress and now it belonged to Jill.

"Caught you," Chip said, smiling at her as he leaned against the doorjamb. "Were you afraid someone had stolen it?"

"I just wanted to see it again. Oh, Chip, it's so lovely. Please let me say thank you just one more time?"

"No! No! No! You wore out my ear with your thank you's. Come back to bed. It's chilly. You mustn't catch cold. You're a famous artist."

"I am not."

"Well, almost. Move it, my sweet. Do you want to have your picture taken tomorrow looking half-asleep?"

"I don't want it taken at all."

"Walk or be carried back to bed. Those are your choices."

"I'm going! Just let me put this dress away."

"I'm wide awake now myself. And tense, terribly tense. What do you suppose I should do about that, Jill?"

"Oh, we'll think of something," she said, linking her arm through his. "Warm milk? A brandy?"

"Three strikes and you're out."

"Trust me, Chandler. Trust me."

The next morning, Chip handed Jill his car keys.

"What are these for?" she asked.

"I don't want you driving that heap of yours. I'll take it and you use my car."

"No. No way. No." She shook her head vigorously. "I refuse."

"Dammit, Jill!"

"Dammit, Chip!"

"Woman, you are going to put me in an early grave!" he roared, snatching the keys out of her hand.

"Tough tootsies," she said, shrugging.

"I'm really bugged at you, Jill Tinsley, but it will have to go on hold so I can kiss you good-bye because I don't have time to be mad *and* kiss you. Get it?"

"Got it."

He kissed her very, very thoroughly, and they were both smiling when they reluctantly ended the embrace.

"Smile pretty for the camera," he said.

"Yuck."

"You're wearing your hair loose, aren't you?"

"I hadn't really thought about it."

"I'd like you to. You'll look like an angel. Bye, babe. I'll see you tonight. Don't forget to get your blood test and drive carefully. And remember you love me."

"I will do all of the above. I do love you, Chip."

"And I love you. Oh, remind me when I get home that I'm mad as hell at you about the car. I'll probably forget."

She laughed. "Okay. I'll write myself a note."

She leaned against the front door after Chip had hurried off, and stared dreamily at the ceiling. Goodness, how she did love that man, she thought. He had changed her life completely. Not just with material things, but with an intangible quality of peace and happiness. He was her life, her reason for being.

Somehow, she thought, she would gain the sophistication and self-confidence she needed to function in his world. She wanted him to be proud of her wherever they went. She had to know how to act, become someone who should be wearing pretty yellow chiffon dresses.

"How do I do that?" she said, throwing up her hands. "How will I learn?"

Hours later, she returned from her photography session and went upstairs to change out of her dress. The photographer had been nice enough, she supposed, but she had been so tense, it had taken longer than expected to get the effect he wanted. She had sat under the glaring, hot lights until her back ached and her smile felt wooden. When finally satisfied, the photographer had suggested she investigate the possibility of doing hair-product commercials, to which she had replied emphatically, "No!"

Her next stop had been the doctor's office, and the blood test had been completed after an hour's wait in the crowded reception room.

Clad in her ever-so-comfortable jeans and a sweater, she lit a fire and curled up in the corner of the sofa with her new sketch pad. She mentally catalogued everyone she had seen that day, but there had been no one with that special something that made a person memorable. Instead, she drew a picture of Cataledge, smiling as the furry pet came alive on the page.

The sound of Chip's key in the door brought her to her feet and rushing into his arms, kissing him before he had a chance to speak.

"Hello to you too," he said, when he raised his head.

"Hi. Don't forget that you're mad at me."

"Oh, yes, that's right. You're a very good secretary."

"We're having leftovers for dinner."

"I hate leftovers. They always taste like they were left over from World War II."

"Too bad. That's what's on the menu."

"That fire looks great. I'm cold down to my toes." He shrugged out of his coat and pulled her by the hand into the living room. "Hey, Cataledge, how did you get there?" he said, picking up the sketch pad off the sofa.

"I was just playing around because I didn't see anyone today that I wanted to draw."

"This is very good, Jill," Chip said, sinking onto the sofa and patting the cushion next to him. "Sit. I missed you. Listen, why don't you call Kellis tomorrow and ask if you can include some animals in your selections?"

"Who would pay money for a picture of a cat?"

"Someone who's crazy about cats. Call him, okay?"

"Sure." She paused. "Chip, I have to get out and around so I can see people."

"I know, but I want some boundaries set as to where you go or I'll worry myself into fifteen ulcers."

"All right. Ready for leftovers?"

"No. Let's send out for a pizza."

"We can't waste all that food!"

"Damn. Did you get your blood test?"

"Yes."

"Would Friday be suitable for you to become Mrs. William Robert Chandler, Jr.?"

"That sounds wonderful, Chip."

"Would you prefer to use Jill Tinsley as your professional name at the gallery?"

"No, of course not."

"Good, I'm glad. I want the whole world to know you're my wife."

"You might not say that after March first."

"Ah, babe, the public is going to love your work, you'll see. If I asked you to do something for me, would you? No questions asked?"

"I don't know."

"If it meant a great deal to me? Would make me a very happy man? Bring an everlasting smile to my face?"

"For heaven's sake, what is it?"

"Throw out the leftovers!" he said, dissolving in a fit of laughter.

She punched him on the arm.

They had pizza for dinner.

Eight

The week fell into a pattern that worked well for Jill and provided little worry for Chip. Each morning at breakfast she would tell him where she was headed in her search for interesting subjects to draw, then would call him at the office when she returned home.

Mr. Kellis had suggested she limit the number of animal pictures to five until they saw how they were received by the public. She drew a squirrel and later an Irish setter she had seen near the house. She also completed a drawing of an enchanting Oriental child, and one of an old man wearing a faded sea captain's hat.

She had dinner on the table when Chip came home from work, and their evenings were spent in front of the fire chatting, or reading, or watching television, or simply sitting close together in comfortable silence. At night in the big bed they reached for each other and soared to their private heaven time and again.

When the alarm sounded on Friday morning, Chip

shut it off with a mumbled expletive and burrowed into his pillow.

"Oh, Lord!" Jill shrieked, sitting bolt upright. "I'm getting married today!"

"Fancy that," Chip said, "so am I. Small world, huh?"

"I'm a nervous wreck. I'll probably say 'I don't' instead of 'I do.' "

"Hush, funny girl." He scooped her up and settled her on top of him. "It will all go perfectly fine. Ummm, your hair is swishing over us like a waterfall. You feel so good, so soft."

She lowered her head and drazed her tongue across his lips, then pressed her mouth firmly to his. He moaned softly and she could feel his arousal pressing against her as his hands roamed over her back and the soft slope of her buttocks. She slid lower, drawing moist circles over his chest with her tongue. He caught his breath when she tugged at one of his nipples with her teeth.

"Jill! You're driving me crazy!" he said as she moved on to the taut plane of his stomach.

"What?" she murmured. "Is something wrong?"

For an answer he rolled her over and gazed at her for one long, loving moment before entering her with a powerful thrust.

Their rhythms matched perfectly, as if they could both hear the cadence of an invisible drummer. The tempo increased as tempestuous sensations surged through their bodies and they reached the crescendo.

"Chip!" she cried, clinging to his shoulders as her body seemed to explode into ecstasy.

"Oh, Jill," he moaned, his body trembling over hers. He collapsed onto her, burying his face in the fragrant cloud of her hair, then slowly pushed himself up onto his elbows.

"Who taught you to do that stuff?" he said, smiling down at her flushed face.

"You!"

"Yeah, I know, and I love myself for it. You are one helluva woman, Jill Tinsley. And today, this very day, you become Jill Chandler. Oh, you feel good. Maybe I'll just stay right here."

"Do judges make house calls? Or rather, bed calls?"

"Don't think so." He sighed, then slid off her and pulled her close to his side. "Now! Do you have the plan straight?"

"Chip, we've been over it ten times."

"Humor me."

"You have to go into the office because you have to close an important deal. At ten, you'll come back here and change into your new suit and pick me up to go to the courthouse. I am to have packed my clothes in my suitcase, but only the necessities since you intend to buy me new things when we get to wherever it is we're going. Your sister and her family are driving down from Midland in time to pick up your parents at the airport and meet R.J. and Helen at the courthouse. We're all going out to lunch, and then you and I are driving to the airport. R.J. will feed Cataledge while we are gone until next Tuesday, because your parents are going on to your sister's for a few days."

"Very good. Go to the head of the class. I, myself, am going to the shower. By the way, there are a couple of things for you in that frilly guest room you like so much."

"For me?"

"Yep."

"What are they?"

"Go see!"

She slid off the bed, put on a robe Chip had lent her, and ran down the hall.

"Oh!" She gasped as she entered the room. "Luggage. Beautiful white luggage. Oh, Chip!" she said, spinning around and bumping squarely into his chest. "Ow!"

"Honeymoon luggage," he said. "Like it?"

"I love it!"

"That other box isn't very exciting. It's practical. Your pea jacket is cute as a button over your jeans but doesn't quite make it with yellow chiffon. Go ahead, open it."

It was a coat. The softest, warmest, most beautiful steel-gray coat Jill had ever seen. It had a small fur collar and nipped in at the waist.

"I've never had such a beautiful coat," she whispered, and flung herself into his arms and kissed him soundly.

"She likes it," he said with satisfaction. "Definitely likes it."

"Thank you! Oh, thank you!"

"You're welcome and I'm running late."

"Chip, wait just a second. I wanted to give you something on our wedding day, too, but I couldn't bring myself to spend your money on your own gift, so . . ."

"Jill, don't start that again!"

"I'm not!"

"You don't have to give me anything."

"This is for you," she said solemnly, walking to the closet and taking out a package wrapped in tissue paper.

He brushed back the paper and stared down at the drawing he held.

"An owl," he said in a low voice. "It's an owl. I'll treasure this for the rest of my life. Thank you. Thank you, my love."

"I love you, Chip."

"And I love you. But now, unfortunately, I've got to hustle. If I'm late, R.J. will shoot me on sight. This client is his baby and we're wrapping up a biggy this morning. Then, my sweet, it's honeymoon time."

"Ours or R.J.'s?"

"Ours! He's had dozens already."

She laughed. "Relatively speaking."

"Indeed," Chip said, striding from the room. "The guy is decadent."

Chip managed to gulp a quick cup of coffee and kiss Jill somewhere in the vicinity of her lips before barreling out the front door. She stood alone in the kitchen and smiled down at Cataledge.

This was the day, she thought. A fairy-tale, fantasy day. She would walk out the door as Jill Tinsley and return next week as Mrs. William Robert Chandler, Jr. Jill Chandler. The name was a celebration of sound, tangible evidence that she loved and was loved in return. She no longer stood alone.

She took a long, leisurely bath, then shampooed her hair. She blow-dried it and brushed it until it glowed in an ebony cascade down her back. At last she floated the yellow chiffon dress over her head and stepped into the matching shoes.

A gentle smile came to her lips as she gazed at her reflection in the mirror. She was beautiful. For the first time in her life, she was beautiful.

Hearing Chip's key in the front door, she walked to the top of the stairs. As if sensing her presence he looked up, his hand that had lifted to unbutton his coat stopping in midair. Neither moved nor hardly breathed as a spell seemed to weave around them. An eternity passed before Chip spoke, his voice choked with emotion.

"You are my wife. You are my life," he said. "I will love and cherish you until the day I die."

He walked slowly up the stairs to her, their gazes still locked together. He cupped her face in his hands and kissed her lightly, fleetingly, then strode down the hall to their room. Jill pressed her fingertips to her lips and blinked back tears of happiness before walking down the stairs on trembling legs.

"Do you have the rings, R.J.?" Chip asked.

"Yes."

"You sure?"

"Yes, Chipper, I have the rings."

"Oh. Doesn't Jill look sensational?"

"Pretty as a picture."

"Where in the hell is that judge?"

"He'll be here, buddy. Relax."

"R.J., do you have—"

"Chip, I've got the damn rings!"

"We have powdered our noses and returned," Helen said as she and Jill joined the two men.

"My bouquet is so pretty," Jill said. "Yellow rosebuds and baby's breath. Thank you so much, Helen."

"I wanted to do it, honey. I've waited a long time to see one of my boys married. My next mission in life will be to see R.J. bouncing babies on his knee."

R.J. laughed. "No way. With Chip out of the picture now, I've got an open field on all the young ladies of Detroit. I plan to enjoy."

"Shame on you," Helen said.

Suddenly the group was descended upon by a smiling throng that turned out to be William and Edith Chandler, Chip's parents, and his sister, brother-in-law, and three young nieces. To Jill it was a blur of faces, endless hugs and kisses, and her mind was whirling.

"Chandler wedding?" a woman said, poking her head out of a door.

"Yes!" Chip yelled.

"You may come in to the judge's chambers now."

"Oh, no, where are the rings?" R.J. said, slapping his pockets and then whooping with laughter as Chip turned pale.

The ceremony was short and the judge's deep voice rumbled through the air like thousands of buzzing bees. Jill felt she was in another world and blinked in surprise when Chip slipped the gold ring on her finger. Her hand trembling, she repeated the ritual with him and heard only the final statement made by the judge.

"Friends," he said, "may I present to you, Mister and Mrs. William Robert Chandler, Jr."

"Oh-h-h," Edith said, bursting into tears.

"Hello, Mrs. Chandler," Chip said, and kissed Jill soundly.

"My turn," R.J. said.

"Make it quick," Chip growled, "or this judge is going to be hearing my trial for murder. Yours."

The judge laughed heartily and shook the newlyweds' hands. Documents were signed, and the next thing Jill knew she was in Chip's car heading for the restaurant.

"We're married," she said, looking at the ring on her hand. "We're married? Chip, I missed the whole thing. I was in a time warp or something."

"Well, I assure you it was all very proper and legal."

"Did I say, 'I do'?"

"Yep, and you will every chance I get."

The restaurant in Grosse Pointe was elegant, with crystal chandeliers and linen tablecloths. Although it was very crowded, the group was led immediately to a reserved table. Chip ordered two bottles of champagne, then disappeared. When he returned he nodded to R.J. as he sat down next to Jill. A few minutes later, a man stepped up to a microphone at the far end of the dance floor and asked for everyone's attention.

"As you probably know," he said, "we have dancing here in the evenings. Well, we've had a request for one dance this afternoon. There is a brand-new bride with us who had a lovely fantasy and we're going to help make it come true. This is your dance, Jill. May you and Chip have many years of happiness together."

"Oh, Chip," Jill whispered.

"May I have this dance, Mrs. Chandler," he asked softly, as the pianist began playing a classic love song.

As if on her cloud of yellow chiffon, Jill was swept into Chip's arms and they glided across the floor together. It was everything, and more, that she had ever dreamed about. Tears spilled onto her cheeks and Chip tenderly kissed them away. When the song ended, the other diners applauded as the radiant couple walked hand in hand back to their table.

"That was something," said R.J., who seemed to have something caught in his throat.

"I'll cry for a year," Helen said. "Forgive me, Chip, for ever saying you aren't romantic. That was beautiful."

"That's my son," William Chandler said proudly.

"He inherited his romantic nature from *me*," Edith said.

"Thank you. Oh, thank you, Chip," Jill said, burying her face in his shoulder.

Chip simply smiled and looked very, very pleased with himself.

After lunch, Chip brought Jill's cranberry wool dress in from the car and she changed in the ladies' room. After one more round of hugs and handshakes, she and Chip headed for the airport. He pulled airline tickets out of his pocket and handed them to her.

"Florida?" she said.

"Now, before you panic, no, we are not spending our honeymoon with my parents, since they'll be safely tucked away in Midland. This is our trip, babe. Yours and mine."

It was sand and surf and sunshine. It was love-making beyond description in all its splendor and beauty, and strolls in the moonlight. It was shopping for clothes and souvenirs and eating fancy meals in elegant restaurants. It was ecstasy.

* * *

Late Tuesday night Chip opened the front door to their home in Westland and, with a dramatic sweep of his arms, scooped Jill up and carried her across the threshhold.

"Ta-*da*," he said, setting her on her feet. "We're home. Damn, it's cold in this town. Let's go back to Florida."

"That sounds fine to me. Oh, hello, Cataledge." She picked up the cat. "How are you, sweetheart? Did you like R.J.?"

"It would seem so," Chip said, picking up a note off the table in the entryway. "R.J. says here that Cataledge and the kittens were thrilled to see him every time he came over. Oh, and Mr. Kellis wants you to call him."

"I wonder why?"

"Probably some detail about the exhibit. I'll go bring in the luggage. I swear, it is so damn cold in this city!"

As soon as Chip had left for the office the next morning, Jill called the gallery and asked to speak to Mr. Kellis, who came on the line immediately.

"Good morning, Jill," he said. "I trust you and Chip had a good trip?"

"Lovely, thank you."

"Well, I have nice news for you myself. Four of your drawings have sold already."

"Pardon me?"

"One of my customers who lives in London came through town and stopped in. I showed him your work and he loved it. He chose four from this group I have here. They're being packed for shipping right now."

"I'm overwhelmed, Mr. Kellis. I really am."

"I told you I wasn't out of my mind, young lady," he said, laughing. "I will, however, need four additional drawings from you now. I have the wall space all coordinated and must have thirty-two drawings."

"Yes, fine. I'll get right to work."

"Good. Congratulations, Jill. You're on your way to a fantastic career."

"Thank you, Mr. Kellis," she said, slowly replacing the receiver.

It was unbelievable, she thought, shaking her head slightly. Four of her drawings had already sold? She had to tell Chip! No, she wasn't going to be the kind of wife who called her husband at the office every two minutes. She'd share her news tonight when he came home. She was an artist! An artist with talent, who created drawings that people wanted to display in their homes! Every dream she had ever had was coming true because of one man, Chip Chandler. Her Chip. Her husband, for as long as they both shall live.

She got to her feet and hurried to the closet for her jacket. She had to get busy! she thought. Mr. Kellis needed even more work from her than planned and she hadn't accomplished that much before the wedding. She knew what areas of the city Chip considered safe enough for her to roam around in, and she'd be back in plenty of time to fix his dinner. She was really an artist!

The day, in spite of its glorious beginning, went downhill very quickly. Not five miles from the house, the panel truck got a flat tire and Jill had to limp into the nearest gas station in the rickety vehicle. She spent the next hour shivering in the drafty office while the tire was patched and she could resume her travels.

Her next stop was a large library where she wandered around, looking for interesting subjects to draw. A beautiful baby sleeping in a stroller caught her eye, but before she could do more than start the sketch, the infant woke and began to wail, and was immediately whisked out of the room by its mother.

A smiling, round-faced priest said he would be delighted to be a model but simply did not have the time. An old man accused her of being a Communist spy, and a teenage boy said he was ditching school and wanted "no evidence on paper, lady." No one in Detroit, Michigan, it would seem, wanted their portrait drawn.

In the middle of the afternoon, Jill gave up and headed home with her sketch pad of blank pages. A little over two miles from the house, the patched tire gave up the ghost and she guided the listing truck to the curb. She locked the door, gathered her art supplies, and started the cold trek home. Her teeth started to chatter before she had gone a block.

Chilled to the bone, she sighed with relief when she turned onto her and Chip's street.

"Uh-oh," she said, seeing Chip's car in the driveway. "I think I'm in trouble."

That was putting it mildly.

"Where in the hell have you been?" Chip roared the instant she stepped into the house.

"Don't you dare yell at me!" she shouted. "Just don't you dare! I've had a lousy, crummy, rotten day. Two, count them, two flat tires, and no one would let me draw his picture, and I'm cold, and you're hollering like a big bully! Shut up, Chip Chandler!"

"I've been calling you since this morning!" he bellowed. "I finally got so worried I came home to see if you were all right. I was nearly out of my mind and— Two flat tires?"

"Yes, dammit. That stupid truck is parked a million miles from here and I had to walk home. I suppose next you're going to scream your head off because dinner isn't ready. Well, too bad because I don't care."

"Oh, Jill," he said, pulling her close. "You're freezing. Get out of that coat and tell me what happened."

She set her things on the table and allowed Chip to pull off her coat. She was a breath away from bursting into tears and sniffled continually to halt the flow of rapidly building sobs.

"You're really chilled, babe," he said. "Go up and take a shower while I light a fire in the living room. I'm sorry I yelled. It's just that I was so worried. Go on upstairs, okay?"

Nodding, she did as she was told, sniffling her way through the otherwise silent exit.

"What's wrong with your nose?" Chip asked when she was halfway up the stairs. "Did you catch cold out there when that damn truck of yours died?"

"Oh-h-h," she wailed, bursting into tears and running up the stairs and down the hall.

"Now what in the hell did I do?" he yelled. "I said I was sorry!"

He lit the fire and paced the living room until Jill reappeared fifteen minutes later.

"Hi," he said, smiling weakly. "Feeling better?"

"No. Yes. I guess so," she said, walking past him and flopping onto the sofa.

"What happened?"

"Okay, here it is. Mr. Kellis said four of my drawings have sold already to a man from London. Oh, Chip, I was so excited. It's come true, don't you see? People like my work. They do! I'm an artist just like you said."

"Jill," he said, sitting down next to her, "that's wonderful! I'm so happy for you."

"Wait. There's more. Mr. Kellis wants four additional drawings to replace those and today I accomplished nothing. Nothing! Except freezing to death and wiping out my truck. I'm running out of time, Chip. I've got so much work to do before that exhibit and everything is going wrong. I was going to unpack our luggage today and it's still sitting there, and dinner isn't even ready."

"Well," he said, grinning at her, "you certainly aren't bored anymore."

"This isn't funny. I've got to get those drawings done."

"Okay, calm down. The first thing is to get you a car. I'll have the truck towed in and we'll trade it off for whatever we can get. You just tell me where you left it. In the meantime, you can take me to work tomorrow and use mine, then pick me up later. Don't worry about meals and junk. You concentrate on those pictures. Jill, I'm so proud of you. Just think, it's coming true. You're an artist, babe."

"I know and I was so thrilled. But then I panicked because now I have so much to do and I've never worked under this kind of pressure before. I can't create interesting subjects in my mind, I have to see them and, of course, ask their permission to be drawn."

"Don't worry, you'll make the deadline. Now let's go out for spaghetti. There's a cozy little Italian restaurant a few miles from here. Tomorrow is a new day. Everything will be fine, you'll see."

But it wasn't.

It was a study in frustration. Jill drove Chip to work and then headed for Mr. Kellis's gallery to deliver the few drawings she had completed. Mr. Kellis was delighted with the work and insisted on giving her a complete tour of the gallery to explain where and how her pictures would be displayed for the exhibit.

The other two artists scheduled to launch their careers along with Jill happened to drop by and Mr. Kellis invited them all to lunch. It was after two o'clock before Jill was able to get away and go to a shopping mall in search of subjects. Her total effort for the day was a sketch of a rabbit she saw in the window of a pet shop.

Driving above the speed limit, she arrived at Chip's office fifteen minutes later than planned, only to be told by R.J. that Chip had bought her a small car, was driving it home, and would meet her back at the house.

"Oh, cripes," she said, turning on her heel and stomping out of the office, leaving a wide-eyed R.J. staring after her.

The car was a cute red compact and she kissed Chip until he said he was going to pass out from lack of oxygen. Her buoyant mood, however, fizzled out when she explained her less than productive day. After a dinner of sandwiches and milk, Chip drove her to another mall, where she managed to convince the mother of freckle-faced three-year-old twins that the children would be excellent subjects for a drawing.

Jill was so exhausted that night that she fell asleep while Chip was in the shower, and he had left for work before she woke the next morning.

Friday was slightly better. Jill called a nursing home and asked permission to visit, explaining her intentions. The home was an hour's drive out of Detroit and it was nearly eight before she pulled into the driveway with two more drawings in her sketch book.

"You're pretty late," Chip said quietly when she entered the house.

"I know, and I'm sorry."

"There's a TV dinner there. Want me to stick it in the oven?"

"I'll do it. Have you eaten?"

"Yeah."

"Okay," she said wearily, walking down the hall to the kitchen.

Chip leaned against the doorjamb and crossed his arms over his chest. He was frowning as he watched Jill set the foil-wrapped tray in the oven.

"Jill," he said, "you're pushing yourself too hard."

"I have a deadline to make."

"I realize that, but you're going to end up sick in bed at this rate. Listen, my sister and brother-in-law have a cabin outside of Midland. We could go up there for the weekend and relax. What do you say?"

"I can't. I need that time to find more subjects for my drawings."

"Jill, I've hardly seen you since we got back from Florida! I'd like some time with my wife. Now you're saying you're going to be busy the entire weekend. What am I supposed to do? Offer to hold your pencils?"

"You're not being fair! I thought you were pleased about how my career was going."

"Of course I am! But you have another career too. You're a married woman as well as an artist," he said, his voice rising.

"Meaning I should have dinner on the table and your slippers by the fire? Dammit, Chip, there are just so many hours in the day. I can't do everything."

"I'm not asking you to. I'd just prefer a little better balance. When are we going to make love? When you can fit it into your schedule?"

"Is that why you're so angry? Because you aren't getting enough?" she yelled.

"Dammit, I didn't say that! Come away with me for the weekend, Jill. Let's close the door on everything and start next week fresh and rested."

"No! I just can't spare the time!"

"For me? You have no time for me? I'm your husband."

"Who supposedly is very enthusiastic about my artistic career, providing of course, that it doesn't inconvenience you in any way. I signed a contract with Mr. Kellis and I intend to honor it."

"I believe that your signature is on our wedding certificate, too, Mrs. Chandler. What about honoring that one?"

"Damn you!" she shouted. "How can you stand there and—"

"I can't!" he said, turning and stalking down the hall. "I'm going out! Enjoy your dinner. Hell, draw a picture of fried chicken and peas!"

Jill cringed as she heard the front door slam, and

then sank onto one of the kitchen chairs. Dear heaven, she thought, what had happened? Everything was crumbling, falling apart. Why couldn't Chip understand that she was desperately short of time and was in a constant state of panic that she wouldn't make her deadline? He knew what pressures she was under. But he had been so hurt and angry. Should she have agreed to go away for the weekend with him? No, she just couldn't spare those hours. She couldn't!

She was so confused. Did Chip prefer her as the broke, starving little creature that had fainted into his arms the day they met? No, that didn't make sense. He was the one who had taken her drawings to Mr. Kellis, the one who had encouraged her to seek out her fantasy and make it reality. She was slowly, slowly taking her place by his side. She felt comfortable, pretty in her new clothes, now met with Mr. Kellis with confidence, and had been warmly received by Chip's family.

"Which Jill do you love, Chip?" she whispered. "The old one, or the one I'm becoming? What do you want from me?"

She spent a restless evening waiting for Chip's return. At each sound of a car she hurried to the window, only to sigh and resume her pacing. Finally at midnight she left a lamp burning in the living room and made her way slowly up the stairs to bed.

A half hour later she heard the front door open and close. Minutes later Chip entered the bedroom. He sat down heavily on the edge of the bed and tugged off his shoes, each landing with a thud on the floor. Then, as if in slow motion, he tipped backward, his head landing within inches of her leg.

"Chip?" she said, sitting up and turning on the light. "Chip, what—He's drunk! William Robert, wake up!" she said, shaking his shoulder.

She scrambled off the bed and ran around to the

other side, planting her hands on her hips as she stared at the inert figure before her. A wave of tenderness washed over her as she saw Chip's tousled hair, his shadow of beard. He was the most beautiful, rumpled-up mess she had ever seen.

She was breathing heavily from exertion after pushing and pulling and finally getting Chip undressed and into bed. He had moaned, groaned, and swore, but not really said anything of intelligence. She crawled back onto her side of the bed and shut off the light.

Now she could sleep, she thought. Chip was home. Such as he was, of course, but he was home. And tomorrow they would sit down and have a calm discussion regarding the changes taking place in their lives. Everything would be fine. It just had to be!

The next morning, Jill moved quietly around the bedroom as she dressed, not wishing to waken a deeply sleeping Chip. In the kitchen she fed Cataledge and then set a huge pot of coffee to drip, deciding Chip would need more than his normal ration.

When the telephone rang, she snatched up the receiver quickly.

"Jill? Mr. Kellis here. Sorry to bother you on a Saturday, but this is important."

"Yes?"

"I just had a call from an art critic who writes for *The New York Times*. He has a few hours layover between planes on his way to San Francisco and asked if I had anything going on here worth writing about. I told him I certainly did, and he's coming over from the airport. I'd like you to drive in and give him an interview."

"Now?"

"Yes. I'll show him your work and then let him talk with you. Don't bother to dress up, just come as you are. This man is interested in artists, not what they're wearing."

"But . . ."

"Can you leave right away?"

"I guess so."

"Good. See you soon. Bye."

Jill replaced the receiver and frowned. Wonderful, she thought. She needed to be home when Chip woke up so they could talk. But as zonked as he was, maybe she could get back before he had slept off the effects of his overindulgence.

She scribbled a note to him, saying she had gone to the gallery, but would return as quickly as possible. She left the note on the kitchen table, grabbed her coat and purse, and ran out the front door.

The New York art critic proved to be knowledgeable, very impressed by Jill's work, and extremely long-winded. He asked her endless questions regarding the subjects in her drawings, her background, child-hood, everything and anything that came to his mind. Mr. Kellis was beaming with pleasure over the attention Jill was receiving, while she tried and failed time and again to bring the interview to an end. She wanted to go home to Chip!

The art critic finally laughed and said he couldn't bring himself to leave without purchasing one of Jill's drawings. She smiled politely and groaned inwardly. That meant yet another one to be replaced by the time of the exhibit.

"You're going to be a big name, Jill," the critic said. "I'll give you a nice write-up in the *Times*. Be pre-pared to hear from the New York galleries, Kellis. I'm betting they'll want to negotiate to show Jill's work."

"We'll be ready," Mr. Kellis said. "Right, Jill?"

"Right," she said miserably.

"Well, how about lunch?" Mr. Kellis said. "It's nearly two o'clock. The morning just disappeared."

"No! No, thank you," she said. "I must be getting home. Chip is waiting for me."

"Ah, newlyweds," he said with a smile. "Run along then. I'll see you next week when you bring me more drawings."

"Yes, of course. Good-bye and thank you both."

It was after three o'clock when Jill turned onto their street, and a knot tightened in her stomach. Chip's car was not in the driveway.

The note on the kitchen table read, "Since you're so busy, I decided to go to the cabin alone. Chip."

"Oh, Chip, no!" she said, clutching the note to her breast. "We've got to talk this through, don't you see? Don't leave me here by myself, Chip Chandler!"

She sank onto a chair and gave way to the tears that had been threatening since the night before. She cried until she was exhausted, then climbed the stairs and flung herself across the bed. She fell into a restless sleep and awoke hours later stiff and chilled.

Unable to face the long evening alone in the quiet house, she went to a movie and stared at the screen with unseeing eyes. Her heart and mind were centered on Chip, and tears kept blurring her vision.

What was he thinking as he sat in the isolated cabin? she wondered sadly. What conclusions would he come to regarding their relationship, their marriage? There had to be a middle ground, a compromise they could reach, but it was impossible if he wasn't there to discuss it. But then what if he didn't come home to her?

Sunday was an endless stretch of hours for Jill. The house seemed to scream at her with its silence and she finally fled the confines of its walls. She found herself near a marina and forced herself to concentrate on her drawings, completing three from the interesting faces along the wharf. As darkness fell she went home, lit a fire in the hearth, and waited for Chip to return.

Nine

Chip ran his hand over his face and opened the car window to allow the chill air to revive his numbed senses. He was exhausted and probably had no business being behind the wheel. His exodus to the cabin had been a disaster. He hadn't slept and had hardly eaten, and when he had returned the keys to his sister, she had bombarded him with questions he had refused to answer.

He had never in his life, he thought gloomily, been so screwed up in his mind. He had been the one who had pushed Jill to go after her art career, and he had been sincerely pleased when she told him the drawings were selling even before the exhibit. And then? Before he knew it, he was being shoved to the sidelines of her life, told she just didn't have the time to spend with him because she had to draw her damn pictures!

"Well, forget it!" he said. "Jill is my wife first and an artist second!" Wasn't she? Or maybe not. He had shown her a world she had only dreamed about and now it was hers for the taking. Did she prefer that one now? Would she just fit him in around the edges as her schedule allowed? He couldn't live like that. He loved her, needed to be with her, to share everything that happened to them. Oh, man, what in the hell was he going to do?

Just before ten o'clock, he turned into the driveway and shut off the ignition. The house was glowing with welcoming lights, and he could think only of Jill as he hurried to the door and inserted the key. When he entered the living room, she rose from the sofa and faced him, the fire crackling its warmth behind her.

"Jill," he said quietly, "I said this to you on the day we were married and I want to say it again. You are my wife. You are my life. I will love and cherish you until the day I die."

"Oh, Chip," she sobbed, rushing into his arms, "I love you so much. Nothing is more important than you, us. Nothing. I'm so sorry about everything."

"I should never have gone away without you, Jill, and I never will again. I can't understand what's going on in my head. It's like a tug-of-war, back and forth. I want you to have your dream. I do! But I'm so afraid of losing you to it. Don't shut me out, Jill. I've waited a lifetime for you and I need you so much."

"My dream of being an artist means nothing without you, Chip. I've sat here so many hours going over everything. I have to fulfill my contract with Mr. Kellis, but I'll never sign another one."

"No, don't say that. We'll find a way to have it all. We will. Oh, babe, let me make love to you. Now. This minute. I need to feel you in my arms, know you're here."

"Yes. Yes, Chip."

Upstairs in the big bed, he came to her with almost frantic urgency, as if to reaffirm in his mind that she was his. She gave of herself totally, willingly, and when fatigue claimed him and he slept, she held him in her arms.

In the light of dawn, he reached for her again, gently this time. He kissed and caressed her body until she was awash with desire, pleading with him to quell the flame of passion within her. He came to her slowly, holding himself in check until she was writhing beneath him, wanting, needing what only he could give her. With a glorious thrust of his manhood he answered her plea and carried her with him to the place they both yearned to go to.

As heartbeats quieted they lay entwined in each other's arms, hands resting on moist skin. Chip brushed Jill's hair back from her face and kissed her gently on the forehead.

"I love you," he said.

"And I love you."

"I'm sorry I came home sloshed the other night. I don't blame you for taking off to the gallery the next morning."

"That isn't why I went. I wanted to be here when you woke up so we could talk. But Mr. Kellis phoned and said an art critic from New York wanted to interview me. I had no idea it would take so long. When I got home, you had left for the cabin."

"New York? The big time. How did it go?"

"Fine. He was a nice man. Problem is, he bought one of my drawings and now I'm another one short of the number. Oh, Chip, this whole thing has gotten so out of hand. The critic from New York seemed to feel there would be galleries back there interested in my work."

"I see," Chip said quietly.

"I don't want to think about it. I'm not even close to completing what I need for Mr. Kellis."

"You will. Listen, we'll just tough up and see this through. You take all the time you need and I'll turn into a paragon of patience."

"You?" She smiled.

"Me. I mean it. After the exhibit at Kellis's we'll sit down and decide what your next best step is. Okay? Just go for it, Jill. Get those drawings done any way you have to. I won't say a word, I swear."

"I'd like to go back over to my old neighborhood. There are beautiful faces there, Chip."

"You're pushing your luck." He sighed. "All right. I'll follow you down there this morning and hand you over to Ricky and Slicer for safekeeping. I must be out of my mind."

"They'll take good care of me."

"That creep Ricky stole my hubcaps!"

"Well, he didn't know they were yours! He gave them back, you know."

"Draw fast and get home."

She laughed. "Okay."

"And call me as soon as you get here."

"Yes, sir."

"And let's make love again. Right now."

"You've got it, Chandler."

Chip had his fingers laced behind his head and was staring at the ceiling when R.J. came into his office.

"Hi, Chipper," R.J. said. "How's married life?"

"Complicated."

"Oh? Why?"

"I just delivered my wife to two Mafia trainees, some flake from New York likes Jill's drawings, and I think I'm getting an ulcer. Jill is so busy I may need a name tag so she'll remember who I am. A part of me is thrilled to death that her work is obviously going to make a hit and another part is scared to death."

"What do you mean?" R.J. said, sprawling onto a chair.

"R.J.," Chip said, looking at his friend, "think about it. I'm the one who encouraged Jill to go after her dream about becoming an artist. I'm also the guy who threw the tantrum of the century because she didn't have time to go away with me for the weekend. I don't always behave rationally when it comes to Jill. What if she makes it big? What if I have to continually share her with another world out there?"

"What is Jill saying about all this?"

"She's under a lot of pressure right now because of the deadline for Kellis. We agreed to discuss it thoroughly after the exhibit."

"Sounds fair."

"So, what do I do? Tell her it was fun, but to knock it off and come home where she belongs? Hell, I can't do that. But the thought of seeing her in snatches of time is not appealing. I want my wife back, R.J.!"

"Whew! This is heavy-duty stuff. I'm not exactly an expert on this husband role, Chip, but it seems to me you'll have to keep your mouth shut. When you get right down to it, it will be Jill's decision to make. Women today have their own careers and goals. You saw to it that Jill found hers. I don't think you have the right to demand she give it up."

"I know that."

"Well, if you make her feel guilty, that's a form of demanding. You'll have to back off and let her decide with no influence from you. Just what exactly do you want?"

"I realize Jill needs an outlet for her energies and talent, but not on *this* scale. What do I want? A wife and a baby. Is that too much to ask?"

"I have no idea, buddy. I really don't."

"Can you imagine what Jill would look like pregnant with my child?" Chip said softly. "She'd be the most beautiful woman ever. Jill is mine. I don't want to share her with anyone but our baby. But you're right, I'll keep my mouth shut and leave it up to her. I don't own her. I just love her."

"You're not sorry are you, Chip? I mean, do you

wish you'd fallen out of love with Jill when you were trying to?"

"Lord, no! She's the best thing that ever happened to me and being in love is great. Well, most of the time it's great. There are moments when it's really the pits. I'll tell you, though, I'd hate to go back to those days when I'd wake up next to a woman and have trouble remembering her name. But enough about me. What did you do over the weekend?"

"Hell," R.J. said, pushing himself to his feet, "I can't even remember her name!"

At four that afternoon Helen told Chip that Jill was on the telephone.

"Hell, it's about time!" he roared. Easy, Chandler, he told himself. Patience, man, patience. "Hi, babe," he said into the phone. "How did it go?"

"Fantastic! I got three absolutely marvelous—Why aren't you yelling because you've been worried all day?"

"Worried? Me? When you were with two outstanding citizens like Ricky and Slicer? Don't be silly. Are you home now?"

"Yes, but I'm going to take these drawings over to Mr. Kellis. Okay?"

"Certainly, Jill. Whatever suits your fancy. I'll see you at the house. Bye."

"Bye," Jill said slowly, staring at the receiver for a moment before she replaced it. Was Chip acting strangely? she wondered. Or was she just imagining it? Maybe there had been a client in his office and he couldn't scream at her for not calling sooner. But then again, he *had* said he'd be very patient while she finished the drawings for the exhibit. Well, she didn't have time to think about it now.

She stopped at the store on the way home from the gallery and bought two large steaks and some frozen broccoli. There would be no TV dinners in the Chandler homestead tonight, she thought as she pulled into the driveway next to Chip's car.

"Chip, I'm home!" she called as she entered the house.

"Hello, sweet person," he said, coming out of the den to kiss her. "Those kittens are getting fat. Really obese. What's in the sack?"

"Dinner."

"I'll help you cook. After all, you worked all day just like I did."

"Help me cook?"

"I insist, Jill. I'm a man of the eighties, you know."

"You are?"

"Oh my, yes. I assume equal responsibility around here for all kinds of things."

"You do?"

"Yep, like helping with this meal, for example, and birth control, and—"

"Hold it, bub. We don't use birth control unless I've missed something in the throes of passion."

"Nope, we're just letting the little chips fall where they may. Oh, Lord, what a great pun. Did you get it? Little Chips?"

"Yeah, I got it," she said, eyeing him warily. "Is there a message here?"

"Well, you suddenly have a wingding career, Jill. I just wondered if you might be having second thoughts about getting pregnant right away."

"Are *you* having second thoughts?"

"We're not talking about me. Are we going to eat or not?"

"What? Oh, yes, let's go into the kitchen. Chip, I thought we agreed to have a baby as soon as possible."

"A lot has changed since then," he said, taking the sack and walking down the hall. Say it, Jill, he pleaded silently. Say you still want a baby now. Please, babe!

Oh, help, Jill thought wildly. What did he want her to say? Had he changed his mind about a baby? She was praying she was pregnant already!

"These steaks look great," he said.

"Chip," she said quietly, "please don't play games about something as important as our child. Are you trying to tell me you'd rather wait a while before starting a family?"

"Like I said, we're not talking about me. You're the one who has new obligations and pressures. I'll leave the decision up to you."

"I don't understand you. I can't decide something like that alone! I thought it was all settled anyway. For all I know, I'm pregnant right now. Dammit, Chip, why are you doing this? You said when we made love we went to heaven together. And that that was where our baby would be conceived. You're obviously having qualms about being a father or none of this would even be open for discussion. What will you do if I'm already pregnant? Send it back to the factory?"

"Dammit," he said, grabbing her by the shoulders, "you make it impossible to be fair, and just, and liberated, and all that crap. Okay, fast mouth, here it is, right between the eyes. I want you to have my baby nine months from yesterday. I want you pregnant out to the wall, and next year we'll repeat the process all over again. I'm trying to be a decent man here and give you some space to move around in in the new world you're building for yourself. Well, forget it! You'll be too fat to move out of my sight! If you're not pregnant yet, then, by damn, I'll practice until I get it right. Any questions? Well?"

"I love you," she said, collapsing against his chest. "Don't you ever scare me like that again. I thought you didn't want . . . Oh, Chip, having your baby is the only fantasy I have that hasn't come true."

"It will, babe," he said, claiming her mouth in a searing kiss.

She returned the kiss with total abandon as tears clung to her lashes. How very complicated was this man she loved, she thought dreamily. And how dear, and warm, and wonderful.

Thank heavens, Chip thought as he took a ragged breath. He had blown his plan to be cool and relaxed about the baby and leave it up to Jill, but everything was all right. How he loved this woman.

"Dinner, Mr. Chandler," Jill said breathlessly.

"Certainly, Mrs. Chandler. I'd be glad to help you, but there's a cat sleeping on my foot."

There seemed to be a special tenderness in their lovemaking that night, a gentleness tempering their heightening passions. Such busy days lay ahead, with hours filled with pressures and fatigue. In the euphoria of their union, though, there was only the ecstasy, the soaring pleasure of their flight to their private heaven. They drifted back slowly, neither wishing to return to reality.

The following days were a blur of activity. Jill became increasingly tense as the day of the opening drew near and she still had not completed the required number of drawings. Mr. Kellis had sent press releases along with copies of the catalogue to the Detroit newspapers, and Jill and the other two artists were set upon by reporters for interviews preceding the showing. Jill was frantic over the time lost, but answered all their questions with poise and patience.

Chip no longer asked her where she was going during the day, knowing she was apt to end up anywhere in her quest for subjects to draw. His would-be ulcer, he decided, was better off not knowing where she had gone.

"Jill," he said late one night, "if you don't stop tossing and turning, you're going to wear a hole in the sheets."

"I can't sleep."

"I know, I know." He moaned. "It's two in the morning and you're still bouncing around."

"I'm sorry. I won't move."

"Jill, it's almost over. You gave Kellis the last of the drawings today, right on time. You've got two days just to relax before the opening Saturday night."

"But, Chip, all these critics are coming, and it sounds like Mr. Kellis has invited everyone in Detroit."

"Yes, I know. But babe, please try to sleep. I've got to meet a client in the morning and I'd really like to sound halfway intelligent."

"I won't say another word."

"Thank you."

"Chip?"

"Why me? Yes, Jill?"

"I love you."

"I love you, too, Jill."

Before leaving for work the next morning, Chip stood next to the bed and gazed at Jill as she lay sleeping. A knot tightened in his stomach and he ran his hand through his hair.

He had made it . . . this time, he thought ruefully. He had called on every ounce of patience and understanding he possessed to see Jill through this thing. The drawings were completed. It was over. But was it? Saturday night was her debut and the gallery would be swarming with people clamoring for her work. And it would happen, there was no doubt about it. The advance sales were proof that she was going to be a success. A big success.

Was it really over, or just beginning? he thought, walking slowly down the stairs. Was he actually to have his wife back after Saturday night, or would this way of life continue for them with the exhibits, pressures, deadlines? Could Jill turn her back on her dream to return to him and the child they hoped to have? How long could they survive like this?

When he walked into the office, Helen was reading the newspaper. "This write-up on Jill is great," she said.

"Yeah."

"She's getting such excellent press even before the exhibit has opened."

"Yeah."

"Thanks for getting me an invitation for Saturday night."

"Sure, Helen. No problem."

"What's wrong, Chip?"

"I just wish it was over with, I guess."

"It's been rough for you two, hasn't it?"

"Yes, there's been a lot of pressure. And they're going to be demanding more from her, Helen. I'm not sure I can go through it again. I'm so damn selfish. I want Jill back, with me. I love her so much and I hate sharing her like this."

"I don't mean to intrude," R.J. said from the doorway of his office.

"You're not," Chip said. "I'm just feeling sorry for myself and wishing I could lock Jill in a closet so those big shots can't make their fancy offers tomorrow night."

"You said you and Jill would discuss the future after the exhibit," R.J. said.

"Yeah, I know, but it doesn't take a genius to figure out they're going to want her stuff. They're scrambling for what Kellis has of hers already. She'd be crazy to turn down what's going to be offered to her. I have the career I wanted, worked hard for. Why shouldn't Jill have hers? I'm just not quite sure where I'll fit into the whole thing."

"Are you going to ask her to choose between you and her career, Chipper?" R.J. asked.

Chip looked at R.J. for a long moment, then walked over to the pot of coffee and poured himself some. He picked up the mug, set it down again without drinking, then turned back to Helen and R.J.

"No," he said quietly, "I'll never do that. I said I didn't know if I could go through this again. That isn't true. I'd do anything to be with Jill. Whatever time we get to have together will have to be enough. If she decides to pursue her art career, then I'll wait for her at home until she can get there. I don't sound too macho, I guess, but that's how it is. I love her. I can't bear the thought of losing her or seeing her unhappy. I just love her."

He attempted a smile that failed, then with a slight shake of his head walked into his office and shut the door. R.J. looked at Helen, but neither spoke.

Saturday was clear and cold with no sign of snow in the cloudless sky. Jill had attempted to be light-hearted and cheerful during the long day, but tension permeated the house and conversation was given up as a hopeless cause. After a makeshift dinner, she and Chip went upstairs to dress for the gala opening. She had washed her hair in the morning and while Chip showered she braided it into a thick plait entwined with teal-blue satin ribbons to match her dress. She twisted the coil onto the top of her head and secured it with stick pins.

While she showered, Chip donned his tuxedo, remembering the night he had showed up at Jill's apartment at midnight. It seemed like a lifetime ago, he thought, that he had met the beautiful, green-eyed woman who didn't know where her next meal was coming from. They had shared so much, grown so much. And now? He didn't know. The future was a fog of uncertainties. But he had meant what he said to Helen and R.J. He would stay with Jill no matter what she chose to do.

He slipped his wallet into his pocket and picked his change up off the dresser. As he slipped on his watch, Jill emerged from the bathroom in her slip and walked to the closet for the teal blue gown. Before his eyes she was transformed into a vision of loveliness as the dress floated over her head and clung to her soft, feminine curves.

"You're beautiful," he said. "Absolutely beautiful."

"Thank you." She smiled. "You picked it out, remember?"

"Are you sure you want to be seen with a penguin?"

She laughed. "You'll knock 'em dead. You're gorgeous in that thing."

"I have something for you," he said, taking a small box out of the dresser drawer.

"For me?"

"It's to let you know how proud I am of you and to say congratulations for what's taking place tonight."

"Oh, Chip, how thoughtful. Oh, it's lovely! I don't know what to say!"

"Then don't say anything," he said, kissing her quickly. "Turn around and I'll put it on for you."

The necklace Chip drew out of the velvet box was a single diamond teardrop on a delicate gold chain. He rested his hands on her shoulders after fastening the necklace around her neck, and they gazed at their reflections in the mirror above the dressing table.

"I love you, my darling," he said softly.

"Oh, Chip, I love you so much. You've been so wonderful these past days, so patient, and—"

"It's getting late. Are you ready to go?"

"Yes. Yes, I'm ready."

The parking lot at the gallery was packed with cars and Chip drove around to the back where Mr. Kellis had told him a spot would be reserved for them. Entering the building by the rear door, they removed their coats and handed them to an attendant on duty.

"Listen to the noise," Jill said, gripping Chip's hand. "It must be crowded with people."

"Your public awaits, my sweet," he said, smiling warmly at her. "This is your big night, Jill."

"Stay close to me, okay?"

"Sure. There's nowhere else I ever want to be."

Their eyes met steadily in a gaze that seemed to last forever. She lifted her hand to stroke his cheek, but suddenly Mr. Kellis came swooping down on them.

"Jill!" he boomed. "There you are, and you look stunning. Things are going beautifully. My taggers will be busy tonight."

"Taggers?" Chip asked.

"When a piece of work is sold," Mr. Kellis said, "a gold tag is placed on the card beneath the drawing or sculpture. I have young men on duty to do that and they're called taggers. You keep an eye out for those gold seals, Chip, and watch the number grow. Come along, Jill, there are important people waiting to meet you."

"But . . ." she said, looking anxiously at Chip.

"Go on, babe," he said. "I won't be far away."

He watched as she disappeared down the corridor with Mr. Kellis, then followed them slowly into the main area of the gallery. Throngs of people were milling about, talking and sipping the champagne that was served by uniformed waiters. Everyone was dressed in their finery and the noise level was high, a festive feeling in the air.

Chip wandered around and idly glanced at the work of the other two artists debuting that night, and raised his brows as the taggers placed several more seals on the cards beneath Jill's drawings.

During the next hours, Chip caught only glimpses of Jill as Mr. Kellis steered her toward the important people she was to meet. She was smiling, even laughing at times, and appeared to be having a marvelous time.

A heavy weight of depression settled over Chip and he finally found a quiet corner and leaned against the wall. Earlier he had waved to R.J. and the voluptuous blonde on his arm. Helen had blown Chip a kiss from across the room and he had nodded, forcing a pleasant expression onto his face.

"You must be a proud man tonight, Chip," Mr. Kellis said, coming up to where Chip was standing.

"Yes, I am. Where's Jill?"

"She's over there, talking with one of our biggest patrons. The last of her drawings just sold. She's a huge success and it's only beginning. Soon she'll be able to name her price, maybe even take her work to the big galleries in New York and California."

"I see," Chip said heavily.

"It would require a great deal of travel for her, of course, but since you two don't have any children . . . Well, I'd better mingle. It was a lucky day for us all when you brought that sketch pad of Jill's to me, Chip. Congratulations."

"Thank you."

Chip resumed his position against the wall and drew a shuddering breath. Lucky day? he thought ironically. Not quite. It had turned his world upside down. If he had it all to do over he'd . . . Yeah, he'd bring the sketch pad to Kellis. Jill deserved to have her fantasies come true. And they had. Even the one about the pretty yellow dress.

At midnight, the artists were asked to say a few words and Chip listened absently as the first two expressed their thanks for the splendid evening. He straightened when Jill began to speak.

"Ladies and gentlemen," she said, her voice clear and strong, "I don't have the words to tell you what tonight has meant to me. Very few people live to see their dream come true and mine has, thanks to your generous acceptance of my work. I am an artist, a title I never believed would be mine."

A smattering of applause broke out, but Jill raised her hands in a request for silence.

"However," she continued, "I had another dream, too, and it came true in the love of the most wonderful man I have ever known. I will continue to draw the faces of those I see who have special meaning to me, but with no deadlines or pressures. I have a family that I want to devote my time to. Thank you for everything, and now it's time for me to go home."

A thundering round of applause went up from the throng, and Chip started toward his wife. He stopped several feet in front of her and slowly extended his hand to her. She reached out and placed her hand in his, her tears mirrored by those glistening in Chip's eyes.

"Are you sure, babe?" he asked, his voice hushed and choked with emotion. "Very, very sure?"

"Yes. Oh, yes, Chip."

"Then let's go home, Mrs. Chandler."

"Forever, Mr. Chandler," she said, smiling brightly. "Forever."

A brief announcement appeared in the *Detroit Times* newspaper on December twenty-sixth that year. "Santa Claus outdid himself yesterday when he visited our city. Jill Tinsley Chandler, the highly successful artist, and her husband, Chip Chandler, became the proud parents of twin boys. Mother and sons are reportedly doing fine and the new father was seen handing out cigars. We extend our wishes of health and happiness to all four of them."

THE EDITOR'S CORNER

Next month should be called "Especially Fabulous Reading Month!" Not only is Bantam publishing four marvelous LOVESWEPTS (of course) and Sandra Brown's sensational sequel to **SUNSET EMBRACE, ANOTHER DAWN,** but also we are reissuing Celeste DeBlasis's extraordinary novel, **THE PROUD BREED.**

An excerpt from ANOTHER DAWN follows this Editor's Corner; next month you can look forward to an excerpt from **THE PROUD BREED.** I know you're going to enjoy both of these longer novels very, very much. By the way, some booksellers display books like **ANOTHER DAWN** and **THE PROUD BREED** in general fiction or in special displays in areas of their stores where you might not think to look for them. So, if you don't see these novels right away, do make a special point of asking your bookseller for them.

Now for those Fabulous Four LOVESWEPTS coming next month.

Sara Orwig creates for all of us a mellow, yet thrilling romance, **DEAR MIT,** LOVESWEPT #111. Just think of the nostalgic pleasure of receiving a letter from your very best friend (and very best tormentor) throughout childhood with whom you've lost touch. Then add that in the present that friend is a thoroughly adult male and a very amusing correspondent who hasn't forgotten a thing about you. Now you're ready to put yourself in heroine Marilyn Pearson's place and imagine her response when at last she encounters Colly face-to-face and finds him devastatingly attractive. And the feeling is definitely mutual. "Mellow," "nostalgic," or any other kind of tame emotion flies right out the window then and it's all sparks and fire between them. But their lives have developed along diverse paths and seem impossible to meld—except perhaps when they stand together beneath the old

(continued)

pear tree that was their special childhood spot. . . . Well, we'll keep you guessing about what happens there, but we won't keep you in suspense about our feeling that **DEAR MIT** is one of Sara's most original, funny, and endearing romances ever!

Given your wonderfully warm welcome for Peggy Webb's first romance, **TAMING MAGGIE,** LOVE-SWEPT #106, I know you'll be very pleased to learn that she has another book coming up next month, **BIRDS OF A FEATHER,** LOVESWEPT #112. In this delectable story, young widow Mary Ann Gilcrest finds herself—much to her dismay and her mother's delight—in the midst of a birdwatchers' retreat. But suddenly it isn't such a dismal event; as a matter of fact it becomes a downright wonderful one! And the not-so-simple reason for the change in Mary Ann's view is magnificent Bill Benson. Alas, their days together in the wilderness are over much too soon and they must go their separate ways. Then Bill promises forever, but she can't believe in their future together. Bill's relentless pursuit causes a furor to break out in her hometown . . . and the most charming madness surrounds this wonderful couple in an ending to **BIRDS OF A FEATHER** that you aren't likely to forget!

And next we have a sensitive, most imaginative author joining us, Linda Hampton, with **A MATTER OF MAGIC,** LOVESWEPT #113. Linda's delightful debut book with LOVESWEPT features the most romantic sleight-of-hand from a marvelous hero, Murray Richards. How he impresses heroine Georgette Finlay when he helps her retrieve a pile of dropped packages and then produces a rose from thin air! Georgette feels it is truly providential that they met because she's a talent agent who's been scouting long and hard for a magician. She does a hard sell job on Murray—but he isn't buying! Magic is strictly a hobby for the high-powered executive. No, he wants a far different relationship with Georgette . . . but will he pull it off only by using every trick of the illusionist's trade to weave a spell of sensual enchantment around her? Getting the answer to that question is getting a sure-fire treat in romantic reading!

Be sure to have a box of tissues nearby when you pick up Joan Elliott Pickart's **RAINBOW'S ANGEL**, LOVESWEPT #114, because this lovely story is probably going to bring tears of sentiment and laughter to your eyes. The hero is the debonair R. J. Jenkins from **SUNLIGHT'S PROMISE** and from the moment he lays eyes on Kelly Morgan he's a goner! Their first encounter takes his breath away . . . their next meeting impresses him with her business acumen . . . their third meeting melts his heart. Kelly touches R. J. as no woman ever has with her beauty, brains, courage, and heart. But they have so little time together and R. J. has to make many difficult decisions before he can commit to Kelly, the adoring mother of toddler Sara. **RAINBOW'S ANGEL** is one of Joan's most touching, truly emotional love stories.

We hope you'll agree with us that the four LOVE-SWEPTs along with **ANOTHER DAWN** and **THE PROUD BREED** add up to "Especially Fabulous Reading Month" from Bantam Books.

With every warm wish,

Sincerely,

Carolyn Nichols

Carolyn Nichols
   Editor
LOVESWEPT
Bantam Books, Inc.
666 Fifth Avenue
New York, NY 10103

Jake followed Banner into the living room. He trod lightly, like a convict who had just been granted a stay of execution. She seemed tranquil enough, but he didn't trust her mood. He had meddled in her business when she had made it plain his interference into her personal life was unwelcome. If she wanted to dally with Randy, who was he to stop her?

Then he had kissed her. What had possessed him to kiss her like that this afternoon? He had been mad enough to strangle her, but he had sought another outlet for his emotions, one even more damaging. He wouldn't have been surprised if she had opened fire on him the minute he drove into the yard. Instead she was treating him like a king just returned to the castle.

"Hang your hat on the rack, Jake," she said. "And I don't think you'll need that gunbelt any more tonight."

"Banner, about this afternoon—"

"Never mind about that."

"Let me apologize."

"If you must, apologize to Randy. He hadn't done anything to warrant you pulling a gun on him."

"I intend to apologize to him tomorrow. I don't know what got into me." He spread his hands wide in a helpless gesture. "It's just that Ross told me to protect you, and when I heard you screaming—"

"I understand."

"And about the other—"

"Are you sorry you kissed me, Jake?"

Her face commanded all his attention. It shone pale and creamy in the golden lamplight, surrounded by the dark cloud of her hair. Her eyes were wide with inquiry, as though how he answered her question was of the utmost importance. Her lips were as tremulous and moist as if he had just kissed them.

His answer was no. But he couldn't admit it out loud, so he said nothing. He had behaved like a man possessed this afternoon when he saw Randy's hands on Banner. She was obviously jealous of Priscilla. Jealousy between them was dangerous. And he knew it. And the sooner he called an end to this cozy evening, the better. "I need to be getting—"

"No, wait." She took two rapid steps forward. When he looked at her as though she had taken leave of her senses, she fell back a step. Catching her hands at her waist, she said quickly, "I have a favor to ask. If you . . . if you have the time."

"What is it?"

"In the living room. I have a picture to hang and I wondered if you could help me with it."

He glanced over his shoulder toward the center room. One small lamp was burning in the corner. The room was cast in shadows, as intimate as those in the barn had been. The parlor was also the scene of the kiss that afternoon. Jake was better off not being reminded of that at all.

"I'm not much good at picture hanging," he hedged.

"Oh, well." She made a dismissive little wave with her hand. "You've put in a full day already and it isn't the foreman's job to hang pictures, I suppose."

Hell. Now she thought he didn't want to help her. She looked crestfallen, disappointed that she wouldn't get her picture hung and embarrassed for having asked his help and being turned down.

"I guess it wouldn't take too long, would it?"

"No, no," she said, lifting her head eagerly. "I have everything ready." She brushed past him on her way into the parlor. "I got the hammer and a nail from the barn this afternoon while you were gone. I tried to hang it myself, but couldn't tell if I was getting it in the right spot or not."

She was chattering breathlessly. Jake thought she might be as nervous as he about returning to this room. But she made no effort to turn up the lamp or light another one. Instead she made a beeline for the far wall.

Was this her way of telling him that she had forgiven his behavior that afternoon, that she wasn't afraid to be in an empty house with him long after the sun had gone down? Had everything she had done tonight been a peacemaking gesture? If so, he was grateful to her. They couldn't have gone on much longer without killing each other or . . .

The "or" he would do well not to think about. Especially since she was facing him again.

"I thought I'd hang it on this wall, about here," she said, pointing her finger and cocking her head to one side.

"That would be nice." He felt about as qualified to give advice on hanging a picture as he would be to choose a chapeau in a milliner's shop.

"About eye level?"

"Whose eye level? Yours or mine?"

She laughed. "I see what you mean." She scraped the top of her head with her palm and slid it horizontally until it bumped against his breastbone. "I only come to here on you, don't I?"

When she glanced up at him, his breath caught somewhere between his lungs and his throat. How could he have ever considered this creature with the bewitching eyes and teasing smile a child? He had been with whores who prided themselves on knowing all there was to know about getting a man's blood to the boiling point. But no woman had ever had an impact on him the way this one did. Except perhaps Lydia those months they were together on the wagon train.

His love for her had mellowed since then. He no longer experienced rushes of passionate desire every time he saw her. That summer traveling between Tennessee and Texas, he had been perpetually randy. Desire for Lydia, desire for Priscilla, desire for women, period.

He had been sixteen, the sap of youth flowing sweetly, but painfully, through his body. But that's what he felt like every time he looked at Banner. He felt sixteen again and with no more control over his body than he had then.

Her skirt was rustling against his pants. Her breasts were achingly close to his chest. She smelled too good for it to be legal. He could practically taste her breath as it softly struck his chin. Before he drowned in the swirling depths of her eyes, he said, "Maybe we'd better—"

"Oh, yes," she said briskly. Taking a three-legged stool from in front of an easy chair, she placed it near the wall and, raising her skirt above her ankles, stepped up on it. "The picture is there on the table. Hand it to me, please, then step back and tell me when it looks right."

He picked up the framed picture. "This is pretty."

It was a pastoral scene of horses grazing in a verdant pasture. "I thought it looked like Plum Creek." She glared at him, daring him to say anything derogatory about the name she had selected.

"I didn't say anything."

"No, but I know what you're thinking," she said accusingly. He only smiled benignly and passed her the picture.

She turned her back, raised her arms and positioned the picture. "How does that look?"

"A little lower maybe."

"There?"

"That's about right."

Keeping the picture flat against the wall, she craned her head around. "Are you really judging or are you just trying to get this over with?"

"I'm doing the best I can," he said, acting offended. "If you don't appreciate my help, you can always ask somebody else."

"Like Randy?"

Her taunt was intended as a joke, but Jake took it seriously. His brows gathered into a V above his nose as he took in the picture *she* made perched on that stool, leaning toward the wall with her arms raised. There was a good two inches of lacy petticoat showing above her trim ankles. Her rear end was sticking out. The apron's bow, topping that cute rounded bottom, was a tease no man could resist. The way her breasts poked out in front clearly defined their shape. No, not Randy. Not anybody if Jake could help it.

He considered the placement of the picture with more care this time. "A little to the left if you want it centered." She moved it accordingly. "There. That's perfect."

"All right. The nail will have to go in about six inches higher because of the cord it hangs by. Bring it and the hammer. You can drive it in while I hold the frame."

He did as he was told, straddling the stool and leaning around her. He tried to avoid touching her, adjusting his arms in several positions, none of them satisfactory.

"Just reach up between my arms with one hand and go over the top with the other."

He swallowed and held his breath, trying not to notice her breasts as his hand snaked up between them. He held the nail in place with the other, though that was no small task because he was shaking on the inside.

This was ridiculous! How many woman had he tumbled? Stop acting like a goddamn kid and just get the job done so you can get the hell out of here! he shouted inwardly.

Carefully he drew the hand holding the hammer back. But not carefully enough. His elbow pressed against her side. One of his knees bumped the back of hers. The backs of his knuckles sank into the plumpness of her breasts.

"Excuse me," he muttered.

"That's all right."

He struck the nail, praying it would go into the wall

with only one blow. It didn't. He moved his hand back and struck it again, and again, until he could see progress. Then, in rapid succession, he hit it viciously several times.

"That's good enough," he said gruffly, and withdrew his arms.

"Yes, I think so." Her voice sounded as unsteady as his.

She draped the silken cord around the head of the nail and leaned as far back as she could while still maintaining her balance on the stool.

"How's that?"

"Fine, fine." He laid the hammer on the nearest table and ran his sleeve over his perspiring forehead.

"Is it straight?"

"A little lower on the left."

"There?"

"Not quite."

"There?"

Damn, he cursed silently. He had to get out of here or he was going to explode. He strode forward, wanting to straighten the picture quickly so he could leave and get some much needed air to clear his head. But in his haste, the toe of his boot caught on one of the stool's three legs and it rocked perilously.

Banner squeaked in alarm and flailed her arms.

Life on the trail for so many years had given Jake reflexes as quick as summer lightning. His arms went around her faster than the blink of an eye and anchored her against him. When the stool clattered onto its side, Banner was being held several inches off the floor.

One of Jake's arms was around her waist, the other hand was flattened against her chest. Rather than letting her slide down, he lowered her. His back rounded slightly as he followed her down, bending over her.

But once her feet were safely on the floor, he didn't release her. Jake had spread his legs wide to break her fall. Now Banner's hips were tucked snugly in the notch between his thighs.

His cheek was lying along hers and when her near-
ness and her warmth and her scent got to be too much
for him to resist, he turned his head and nuzzled her
ear with his nose. His arms automatically tightened
around her. He groaned her name.

How could anything that felt so right be so wrong?
Lord, he wanted her. Knowing in his deepest self that
what had happened that other time was an abomination
against decency, he wanted her again. There was no
use lying to himself that he didn't. He had hurt her
once. He had sworn never to again. He had betrayed a
friendship that meant more to him than anything in the
world.

Yet such arguments were burned away like fog in a
noonday sun as his lips moved in her hair and his nose
breathed in the fragrance of the cologne that had been
dabbed on that softest of spots behind her ear.

"Banner, tell me to leave you alone."

"I can't."

She moved her head to one side, giving him access.
His lips touched her neck.

"Don't let this happen again."

"I want you to hold me."

"I want to, I want to."

He moved his hand from her chest up to her neck,
then her chin, until his hand lightly covered her face.
Through parted lips her breath was hot and quick on
his palm.

Like a blind man, he charted each feature of her face
with calloused fingertips suddenly sensitized to capture
each nuance. He smoothed her brows, which he knew
to be raven black and beautifully arched. His fingers
coasted over her cheekbones. They were freckled. He
had come to adore every single freckle. Her nose was
perfect, if a bit impudent.

Her mouth.

His fingers brushed back and forth over her lips.
They were incredibly soft. The warm breaths filtering
through them left his fingers moist.

He pressed his mouth to her cheek, her ear, into her hair.

The hand at her waist opened wide over her midriff. He curled his fingers against the taut flesh. She whimpered. He argued with himself, but there was no stopping his hand from gliding up the corrugated perfection of her ribs and covering her breast. Their moans complemented each other.

Her ripe fullness filled his hand, and against his revolving thumb, the center of her breast tightened into a bead of arousal.

"Jake—"

"Sweet, so sweet."

"This happens sometimes."

"What?"

"That," she answered on a puff of air as his fingers closed around her nipple. "They get that way sometimes . . . when I look at you."

"Good God, Banner, don't tell me that."

"What does it mean?"

"It means I never should have stayed."

"And they won't go down. Not for the longest time. They stay like that, kind of itchy and tingling—"

"Oh, hush."

"—and that's when I wish—"

"What?"

"—that we were in the barn again and you were—"

"Don't say it."

"—inside me."

"Jesus, Banner, stop."

He made a cradle of his palm and laid it along her cheek, gradually turning her head to face him. And as her head turned, so did her body. The fabric of her clothes dragged against his like the tide on the seashore, separate, yet bound.

When their eyes met and locked hungrily, he lowered his mouth to hers. He thrust his tongue deep into her mouth as he pressed her hips against him.

He tore his mouth free. "No, Banner. I hurt you before, remember?"

"Yes, but that wasn't why I was crying."

"Then why?"

"Because it began to feel good and I . . . I thought you'd hate me for the way I was acting."

"No, no," he whispered fervently into her hair.

"You were so . . . big."

"I'm sorry."

"I just didn't expect it to be so . . . and . . . and so . . ."

"Did it feel good to you at all, Banner?"

"Yes, yes. But it was over too soon."

He laid his hard cheek against hers. His breathing was labored, otherwise he didn't move. "Too soon?"

"I felt like something was about to happen, but it didn't."

Jake was stunned. Could it be? He knew whores faked it. He didn't have any experience with decent women. Certainly not with virgins. Never with a virgin. He had never taken anyone he could feel tenderness for.

But tenderness for Banner enveloped him now. He cupped her face between his hands and went searching in her eyes for the truth. He saw no fear there, only a keen desire that matched his own. Making a growling sound deep in his throat, he lowered his head again.

"Hello!" a cheerful voice called out. "Anyone at home?"

Only then did they become aware of the jingle of harnesses and the unmistakable sounds of a wagon being pulled to a halt outside.

"Banner? Where are you?"

It was Lydia.

LOVESWEPT

*Love Stories you'll never forget
by authors you'll always remember*

☐	21603	**Heaven's Price** #1 Sandra Brown	$1.95
☐	21604	**Surrender** #2 Helen Mittermeyer	$1.95
☐	21600	**The Joining Stone** #3 Noelle Berry McCue	$1.95
☐	21601	**Silver Miracles** #4 Fayrene Preston	$1.95
☐	21605	**Matching Wits** #5 Carla Neggers	$1.95
☐	21606	**A Love for All Time** #6 Dorothy Garlock	$1.95
☐	21609	**Hard Drivin' Man** #10 Nancy Carlson	$1.95
☐	21611	**Hunter's Payne** #12 Joan J. Domning	$1.95
☐	21618	**Tiger Lady** #13 Joan Domning	$1.95
☐	21613	**Stormy Vows** #14 Iris Johansen	$1.95
☐	21614	**Brief Delight** #15 Helen Mittermeyer	$1.95

Prices and availability subject to change without notice.

Buy them at your local bookstore or use this handy coupon for ordering:

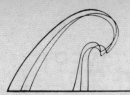

LOVESWEPT

Love Stories you'll never forget by authors you'll always remember

Prices and availability subject to change without notice.

Buy them at your local bookstore or use this handy coupon for ordering:

LOVESWEPT

Love Stories you'll never forget
by authors you'll always remember

LOVESWEPT

Love Stories you'll never forget by authors you'll always remember